"Jordan, there's something I want to tell you."

I looked up at him. "What, Drew? What is it?"

He wrapped his arms tighter around me. "It's . . . it's nothing," he said finally. "Except . . . except that I love you."

"That's not nothing, Drew," I was finally able to answer. "That's a pretty big something."

"I know," he said. "I just want you to remember it, Jordan. No matter what."

How could I forget?

Caprice Romances from Tempo Books

A CAPRICE ROMANCE

Prescription for Love
Judie Rae

TEMPO BOOKS, NEW YORK

PRESCRIPTION FOR LOVE

A Tempo Book / published by arrangement with
the author

PRINTING HISTORY
Tempo Original / June 1984

ISBN: 0-441-67771-1

Tempo Books are published by The Berkley Publishing Group,
200 Madison Avenue, New York, New York 10016.
Tempo Books are registered in the United States Patent Office.
PRINTED IN THE UNITED STATES OF AMERICA

For **Carol, Fran
Judy** and **Stephanie**—

*who share the dream
and helped mine
become reality*

Chapter One

If you ask me, hospital work is the pits. Of course no one did ask me, but I'm telling you anyway. No one ever asks me anything important. Every morning before I leave for school my mom asks, "Did you brush your teeth?" And every morning I ask myself, now *why* did she ask that? Do I have last night's green beans stuck between my canines? Do I have bad breath? Maybe my mouth's lopsided and that's why she notices my teeth so often. And if my mouth *is* lopsided, maybe I kiss funny. *Do* I kiss funny? (I kiss my stuffed bear, Julius, but he doesn't respond.) You see the kind of problems I have?

It all has to do with self-confidence, I know. When they were handing out the self-confidence I was so *un*confident I stood in the body-beautiful line instead, thinking that with a beautiful body no one would notice my assurance level. But unfortunately, by the time I got to the head of the line they were closing up shop. "Sorry," they said, "we're all out of beautiful bodies." That kind of thing happens to me all the time.

Take last week, for example. My dog Oswald and I were standing in the Parks and Recreation rabies-vaccine line. With just two dogs ahead of us, they ran out of vaccine. I had to pay the vet ten bucks for Oswald's shot—the very same vet who charged only two-fifty at the park. You get the picture?

What all this has to do with hospital work is this: About a year ago I realized that I wasn't going to be winning any homecoming-queen awards. I waited around until the ripe old age of fifteen just to make sure I wasn't a late bloomer, but still nothing much happened. What I ended up with was brown hair, brown eyes, average height, and average weight. Dull. Dull. Dull.

Once in a while you see a perfectly ordinary body win the songleader/class-president award, but those are the ordinary bodies with the "Aren't I wonderful anyway!" attitudes. I guess I really did stand in the wrong line. (Why do I learn everything in retrospect?)

Anyway, when this painful recognition dawned on me, I took my average dull and boring figure down to the Regional Occupational Program (ROP) office, which is really the Guidance Counselor's office, separated by a file cabinet, and signed up for vocational training as a nurse's aide. I thought that would prepare me to do something admirable with my life, something to better society. Of course I also had it in mind to start earning money early so I would be well on the way to my first million by the time I hit twenty. I had fantasies of all those beauties in my class someday saying, "Remember Jordan Collins—the blah, uninteresting one? Well, I saw her on the news last night. They say she's the wealthiest woman in the world now."

I also thought it would be a good idea to get out of

school early and get a head start on my dreams. ROP allows you to earn extra school credits for the outside work involved. Of course the best-laid plans of Jordan Collins *always* go astray, so what I ended up with was 180 hours of nurse's training, which put me in touch with bed pans and Miss Piaget.

It also put me in touch with reality, which raised its nasty head and said, "Ordinary Jordan, if you want to be a millionaire, this isn't the way to do it. And if you want to get out of school early, you'll need more than ten credits."

And last, but by no means least, it put me in touch with Drew Richards. Drew was the only boy in my nurse's training program, and if it was a strange place for me to be, it was doubly strange for Drew. On the other hand, I figured maybe he likes bed pans. It was a sure bet he couldn't like Miss Piaget.

Miss Piaget is tall and gray—hey, that rhymes—and is about 140 years old. I think she was a nurse in the days before anesthesia, when all they gave the patient was a slug of whiskey and a bullet to bite.

There is absolutely no funny business in Miss Piaget's class. She wears a silver whistle around her neck on a long chain. I've never heard her actually blow it, but I bet that chain could strangle a kid in four seconds flat.

The very first day of class she started in. "ROP is a vocational training, entry-level program established by the county superintendent of schools. Students are prepared for after-school part-time or full-time jobs, summer employment, and insight into a college major and potential career. Both males and females are encouraged to participate in nontraditional fields. The classes are offered at no cost. Bus tickets are available if needed. This course takes a minimum of ten weeks to learn background material. A minimum of ten practice sessions are required, and another five sessions are necessary to learn proficiencies.''

I looked around the classroom. So far no one had fallen asleep, but no one was looking overly enthusiastic either.

"We will be in class from ten to eleven on Saturday mornings and then at the hospital from twelve to one. Bus transportation will be provided to the hospital and back.''

Saturdays? School on Saturdays? What had I gotten myself into? Why hadn't my counselor told me this. School on Saturdays—they had to be kidding!

Before I had time to complain, Miss Piaget was handing out a three-page syllabus entitled *The Job of Nurse's Aide*. Wait a minute! Maybe I don't want the job. Maybe I should resign. Could unconfident Jordan say that to tall, gray Florence Nightingale who strangles students in her spare time?

I swallowed my fears and vowed to talk to her later, on the phone. That way I could memorize a speech, say it, and hang up before she could argue with me. I glanced at my syllabus. I would have to recognize equipment and supplies. There was some mention of trapezes—they put patients on a trapeze? No wonder so many folks check into a hospital and never check out. What sorts of unknown tortures was I about to learn?

Under "Records" there was this cute little notation: "Does intake and output." I *know* what that means. If they think for one second I'm going to go around measuring someone else's intake and output, they've got another think coming.

It got worse. So much worse I can't say. Collections and treatments and different types of temperature readings. Forget it. I decided I'd rather go into something safe, something like fashion merchandising or bank telling or even electronics.

I was well on my way to quitting when Drew Richards changed my mind. It wasn't fickleness on my part, honest. It was a pure unadulterated desire to get to know him better. You see, he *talked* to me. Never in the history of my high-school career had any boy had more than the most limited of conversations with me: "Whaddaya got for number two on the geometry test, Collins?" "Can ya move over, I need to get into my locker."

But now suddenly here was this person, this boy, holding an extended dialogue with me. I was doing my best to hold up my end of the banter, but a number of unrelated thoughts kept running through my head:

He sure is cute. Probably has a girlfriend. What a nerd he must be—a boy in nurse's training. Female chauvinist.

"I'm sorry. Would I what?"

"I said would you like to study with me later? I was watching you in class and you looked sort of lost."

I just stared at him.

"You know, maybe you should have your ears checked. I bet we could do it for nothing through the program. You haven't heard a word I said. My name's Drew. Drew Richards. You're Jordan, right? I think the class is going to be great, don't you?"

"Yeah, great."

Had pure unadulterated desire committed me? No doubt. Suddenly I was mad at myself. What had happened to all my high ideals, my mercenary standards of making millions and leaving my classmates behind in the dust? Was I throwing it all away on the possibility, the mere chance of a relationship with this boy?

I looked down at my syllabus again. It might be bad, but nothing I couldn't handle. And it didn't mean I actually had to become a nurse. I could have it all. Nurse's training was but a stepping stone, the first brick down the yellow brick road to fame and fortune. I *could* have it all. I'd be a doctor, a famous heart surgeon perhaps.

I smiled at Drew. He was tan and very blond, probably a skier. Of course he'd be a skier—I hate snow. "Why, I'd love to study with you," I said sweetly. "My plans include memorizing all this stuff immediately."

His baby blues smiled back at me, a confused, "What for?" smile.

For now, I'd keep him guessing.

Chapter Two

"The reason I'm in nurse's training," Drew explained to me after class, "is because my first choice, emergency medical training, was closed. I guess I registered too late." He took a last sip of his soda and made a slurpy, squeaky sound, the kind my mother always gives me the "Did you have to?" look for. The noise sort of accentuated his misery. He was very cute even though he was miserable. His blond hair sort of drooped down over his eyes, and he kept pushing it out of the way with his hand.

I couldn't believe I was having a Coke on such a beautiful afternoon with such a gorgeous creature. "I want to be a doctor," he continued. "I had hoped to take emergency training 'cause you get to do on-the-spot work in the emergency room."

I thought of all the doctors I had been to in my lifetime and gave a silent prayer of thanks that none of them had looked like Drew. I couldn't imagine having a thing of such beauty staring down my throat in search of infected tonsils.

Now that I had made up my mind to make my millions as a doctor, a terrible thought occurred to me: Did that mean I would be in competition with Drew? Competition for grades, for scholarships, for a spot in medical school? I decided not to tell him about my plans yet. I had the sneaky suspicion he was one of those purists who really wanted to put an end to pain and suffering in the world. My motivation included staying close to him at all costs and eventually showing the 482 other members of the eleventh grade exactly who they had ignored. At any rate, I figured I would have to tread carefully.

Drew and I were at Bob's, the home of the famous Big Boy hamburger, and not one friend, acquaintance, or vaguely familiar form walked in. How could that be? My first actual sit-down-and-talk-awhile date with a guy, and no one was around to witness it.

Carrie and Pam would never believe me. I decided I wouldn't tell them anyway—at least not yet. After all, I might just be hallucinating or suffering ROP withdrawals or something. Maybe none of this was really happening.

"You're so quiet," he said. "I like girls who listen, but I also like them to talk to me."

Was that my cue to mouth off? What should I say? Tell him a joke, recite the prologue to *The Canterbury Tales*, what? Nothing in life had prepared me for this moment.

"I guess I'm just the shy type," I said. Carrie and Pam would be rolling on the floor if they heard that one. After all, who'd gotten thrown out of the Twin Oaks Theatre for being too loud and silly? Who'd been asked to leave Sunday school until she could compose herself? (In my own defense, it was Pam who drew the funny picture of Sara Long mooning over Kenny Stuart.)

"Why did you enroll in nurse's training?" Drew asked me.

Now what? I couldn't tell him about my "I'll show them" plans. He'd think I was nuts.

"I guess I've always wanted to learn more about nursing," I lied, and immediately realized how easy it was. Was this the start of my career as an untruthful person? And all for the questionable love of the guy who might someday beat me out of a place at the operating table? The thought of being his assistant made me sick. (I wasn't *that* lacking in confidence.)

Nurse, scalpel please.

Get your own scalpel, Doc. Who do you think I am, your little helper?

If my thoughts were known, not only Drew but Miss Piaget would be done with me forever. Is that any way for a nurse to talk?

Drew flipped a quarter on the table as a tip for our drinks and picked up my books as well as his own. I decided it was time to bid my farewells. I wanted to give myself a little breathing room. I definitely needed some time to think things through, think about what I was getting in to.

"Thanks for the Coke," I said, reaching over to take my books from him. "Guess I'd better get home and read up on systolic blood pressure."

"You're pretty serious about all this, aren't you? Can I walk you home?"

I should have said yes. I know I should have said yes. Any normal, in-her-right-mind girl would have said yes.

"No thanks," I told him. "I have to stop at the market and get some things for my family." Another fib. This was getting dangerous. To take care of my tall tale I did stop in at Lucky's for a box of granola bars. Technically they were for me, but if I shared them with the kids they would then belong to the Collins family as a whole. I took out a couple of bars for myself and left the rest for Jimmy and Jessica to fight over.

On the walk home I munched and thought, munched and thought. What had I gotten myself into? I was in nurse's training, which I would probably hate, preparing to become a doctor, and I hate blood, and now I was involved or sort of involved with Drew Richards, who appeared to be dedicated, honest, and supremely self-confident—all the things I'm not.

It may be true that opposites attract; but I had the feeling if Drew knew *how* opposite, he'd drop me just like our waitress at Bob's had dropped a chocolate milkshake: splatter, squish, splat. There went my love life, a formless blob spreading over the linoleum of life, lost before the sweet nectar of the gods had touched my lips. Gosh, I'm poetic. No. I couldn't let that happen. I decided to keep up my little charade and see what developed.

But, I decided, if anyone asks me to empty a bed pan, it's all over.

Chapter Three

As I rounded the corner, I could hear the twins outside fighting over something. And as I got closer, I could see that the object in question was Oswald.

"You walked him yesterday," Jessica screamed.

"Well, so what? You wanted to ride bikes with Penny so I let *your* friend borrow *my* bike. Doesn't that count for something?"

Poor Oswald was taking it all in stride, but I wondered if the shouting wasn't hurting his ears. I reached into the grocery bag for two granola bars and held them out to the kids. "Look what I bought you." They both ran toward me, their argument forgotten. "Oswald doesn't want to walk anyway," I said. "He'd rather sleep." Oswald looked hopefully at the twins, realized they weren't about to share their food, then strolled off to lie down in the sun.

Jessica and Jimmy are ten and are exactly the same height. Jessica wears her hair short, so from the back it's hard to tell the two of them apart. Even from the front it's sometimes hard for strangers, but with a really close look you can see that Jessica's features are rounder and more feminine than Jimmy's.

They both have big brown eyes and cute little turned-up noses. Jimmy's usually runs because of his allergies. Jessica is very bossy and is always making plans for the two of them. That used to be all right with Jimmy, but lately he's begun to assert himself more. I guess he's tired of being told what to do by his sister.

I think maybe Jessica is hurt and angry. She certainly doesn't seem to understand why her best buddy has suddenly started deserting her in favor of boys. It must be especially hard because she builds neat forts and plays basketball better than any of Jimmy's friends.

Mostly the twins and I get along, but sometimes they do really stupid things that make me mad. Last week Jessica and her friend Penny got into my cosmetics and used up half my eyeliner.

It must be tough being a twin. I'm glad it didn't happen to me, although it easily could have. My mother is a twin, and my aunt has twin boys. Maybe I'll go into genetic engineering, as long as I'm into medicine now, and figure out *my* chances of producing look-alikes.

I put my books down on the kitchen table and sneaked a peek in the oven at dinner.

"It's a roast," Mom said, coming in from the garage with a load of wash. "How was your nursing class?"

"I think it's going to be a lot of work. And it's held on Saturdays. *All day* Saturday. Next week we get our assignment."

"Assignment?"

"Yes. We're assigned to a certain section of the hospital to practice our nursing-care responsibilities. You know—pediatrics, post-op, geriatrics."

"Sounds interesting, dear." Mom set the laundry basket down on the chair and started folding clothes. "Are you sure you're strong enough for nursing? You'll probably be required to lift patients in and out of wheelchairs and baths."

"I think we learn how to do it correctly, so we don't break our backs," I said. "And anyway, you get to hang from a trapeze if you goof up."

Mom looked at me as if she had no idea what I was talking about. "Well, let's hope you don't goof up," she finally said, handing me a pile of dark clothes. Carrie's mom makes Carrie wash all her own clothes. So far, my mom hasn't thought of that, thank goodness. Or maybe she has and thought again. Last summer when she and the twins went to visit Grandpa in Illinois, I stayed home and took care of the house and Daddy. I washed Dad's clothes with my red sweatsuit, and he ended up with pink undershirts. How was I supposed to know about separating the clothes? It's not like I spend a lot of time studying the commercials.

"When's dinner?"

"As soon as your father comes home."

I took my clothes and books down the hall to my bedroom, the last room on the left. Jessica's is next to mine, and Jimmy's is the one next to Mom and Dad's. We're all sort of crowded into that one part of the house. Mom and Dad would like to have a den, I know, but none of us get along well enough to share a room. Meanwhile, Mom has screened off one section of the garage for her pottery, and Dad has his desk tucked into a corner of their bedroom.

I love my room, except for the fact that it doesn't have a phone. Pam and Carrie both have their own phones. I have to stand in the hall if I want to talk or else head for Mom and Dad's room if I want privacy. Last week I got shooed out of there because I put my bare feet on the bedspread. How was I supposed to know they were dirty? The way Mom carried on, you would have thought I'd stepped in mud or something. As soon as I'm making millions, I'm going to order my own telephone.

I kicked off my shoes, sat down on my bed, and pulled out the syllabus Miss Piaget had given us. There was a lot of material to learn. I wondered how I'd ever cover it all and still keep up with my regular studies.

Plus, with my Saturdays devoted to nurse's training, when would I have time for any socializing? I don't have a whole lot of friends, but I'd like to keep the ones I do have. That requires a certain amount of time. If I socialize in church, I get thrown out and then Mom gets mad. And if I socialize in school, it shows up on my report card. What am I supposed to do?

This additional burden was giving me a terrible headache, or maybe it was the Coke/granola bar combination. It was Friday evening, and my ROP class would meet at the hospital a week from Saturday. That meant I had exactly eight days to decide my future. I could be on my way to fame, fortune, and romance, plus hard work, bed pans, and bandages, or I could be back on the same old safe but boring path.

Did I have a choice? Didn't I have to prove to my classmates *and* myself that Jordan Collins could accomplish something special? But what if they didn't care? What if I hated being a doctor? How would I know until I tried?

These internal conversations I have with myself are really exhausting. I wonder if everyone has them or just me? In any case, I wouldn't know until I tried, which seemed like maybe a lot of work for nothing and I am basically lazy. On the other hand—

"Dinner, Jordan."

My mom is being very nice these days. She must sense my inner turmoil. (I guess it shows.) Either that or she put the twins to work. What other reason could she have had for not making me set the table?

Chapter Four

Pam, Carrie, and I walk home from school every day together except Thursdays, when Pam's mom picks her up for flute lessons. The walk doesn't seem nearly as far or the books as heavy with someone to talk to. Without the two of them to entertain me, I don't know what I'd do. Probably contemplate hitching a ride with my neighbor Tommy Tompkins, a truly desperate measure.

Pam and Carrie have absolutely no interest in ROP. What they do have an interest in is boys. "Did you see Hillary this morning?" Pam said to us. "I can't believe she made cheerleader. I don't think she's that cute, do you?"

"No," Carrie said. "But *she* does." Carrie understands about the self-confidence quotient, or in this instance, the arrogance quotient. Hillary made cheerleader because it never once occurred to her that she wouldn't.

Hillary also made Don Pomerantz's new steady, which is what's really bugging Pam. "I don't see what he sees in her, do you?'' Pam shifted her books from one skinny hip to the other.

"Ours is not to reason why," Carrie answered. Not satisfied with that answer, Pam looked quizzically in my direction.

"Don't ask me," I said. "How would I know what interests Don Pomerantz?" Or any other guy for that matter.

I thought of Drew. Probably my having a Coke with him was just a fluke accident. Someone probably told him I was a genius or something and he was hoping I'd help him down the road to doctorhood. I *am* smart, but the thought made me mad. He can help himself down the road. Who does he think I am—the Wizard of Oz?

Pam started whining. She does that a lot. It's not one of her more attractive habits, but Carrie and I put up with it, I guess because she puts up with our abnormalities. "I hate my haircut," she said. "Mom's hairdresser really butchered me." She reached up and fiddled with her bangs. "Just look at this. Too short to curl. What a disaster!"

"I think your hair looks cute," I said, and immediately regretted my remark. Pam gave me one of her "How could you?" looks.

"I asked Mom if I could stay home this morning, and guess what she told me?" Pam continued.

"She obviously said no," Carrie responded.

"What she said," Pam went on, "was, 'Do you plan on staying home until your hair grows?' My mother is the most unsympathetic person I have ever met in my entire life."

Personally, I sort of like Pam's mom, but I wasn't about to come to her defense. A sense of timing is very important when dealing with Pam.

I guess Carrie's braver than I am. "Oh, your mom isn't

that bad," she said. "At least she doesn't embarrass you in public the way my mom does. *My* mom sings out loud to herself in the grocery store. You can hear her three aisles over. I could die of shame. Let's talk about something else. Even the thought of it embarrasses me." Carrie's peaches-and-cream complexion was turning red. "Did you go to that nurse's training class Friday, Jordan?" she asked.

"Yeah," I answered.

"Yuck! You're kidding. You want to work around vomit and pus and who knows what else?" Pam said, giving me a look of astonishment. It was accentuated by the fact that her bangs were so short they no longer covered her straight dark eyebrows.

Those eyebrows were like sideways exclamation points, further proving what a dummy I was. "I never noticed your eyebrows before," I said meanly. *That* shut her up.

Carrie shook her head. Her soft yellow curls glowed in the sunlight. "There're some good things about nursing, too," she said.

My two best buddies are very different. Carrie is round and blond and cuddly-looking (maybe too cuddly—she is a bit on the chubby side). Pam is dark and angular and sort of sticklike. Jimmy once said she reminded him of a praying mantis. Carrie's more the ladybug type.

"What's it going to be like?" Pam asked. "Are you going to have to disembowel cadavers and throw out old hearts?"

"Gee, you're pleasant," Carrie said.

"I don't think so," I said. "Mostly it's routine stuff. Taking temperatures, giving baths, that kind of junk."

"What if you have to give a guy a bath?" Carrie giggled.

I hadn't thought of that. "I'm not even sure I'm going to continue with the class," I told them. "I'm not sure I'm really nurse material."

"You're just afraid to give a guy a bath, Jordan," Carrie said. "You can't fool us."

"I'm afraid of ruining my grades in my other classes," I admitted. "I'm afraid I'll have to study all the time. And I'm afraid I'll faint if I see something gory."

"Oh, you'll see something gory, all right," Pam said. "My cousin's a doctor, and his medical books are positively gross. They're *full* of gory stuff."

I'm afraid of liking Drew too much and I'm afraid of him not liking me at all, I thought. Of course I didn't say that to Carrie and Pam. Some thoughts are too private to share, even with your best friends.

I said good-bye to the two of them in front of Carrie's house, and walked the rest of the way alone.

The first thing I saw when I entered the kitchen was a message for me on the blackboard. It read: "Jordan, call Drew. 458–4421. Went to market. Love, Mom."

How could she be so casual? *Jordan, call Drew.* I'd never called a boy in my life (except for crank calls), and I wasn't about to start. Maybe she thought Drew was a girl? Drew-anna? No. Impossible. His voice is too deep. If she thought that, Mom's the one who needs her ears checked.

I took an apple from the bowl on the kitchen table and walked down the hall to my room, all the while wondering what he wanted. Of course I wouldn't know unless I called him. Who did he think he was? I bet he has girls calling him all the time. I bet his phone rings off the wall. Well, I wasn't about to join the crowd.

*   *   *

The next thing I knew Mom was shaking me awake. I guess I fell asleep contemplating Drew's phone call. Falling asleep can be a very convenient thing to do, I've discovered. Sometimes, if you sleep long enough, problems sort of resolve themselves.

"Telephone, sweetie," Mom was saying. "And it's dinnertime."

I walked down the hall in a blur. I must have been really tired. School does that to me sometimes; I short out periodically. The smell of Mom's lasagna brought me around again. That and her reminder that there was someone on the phone for me.

"Hello."

"Is this Jordan?"

"It is I." I love answering the phone that way. My English teacher, Mr. Erickson, says "It is I" is technically correct, even though "It's me" is considered okay now, too, because everyone says it.

"Wow! I had to call four different Collinses before I found you. I was about to give up. This is Drew. Drew Richards."

"Oh, hi." How many Drews did he think I knew?

"I saw you at school today and wanted to talk to you, only you were sort of wedged between a tall dark-haired girl and a short blond one."

"Yeah, I'm usually wedged between those two."

"Did you think about the two of us studying together? I've gone over some of those questions Piaget gave us, and they're really tough. I thought maybe we could work on answering them tomorrow after school in the library. Okay with you?"

I had the funny feeling Drew was about to make up my mind for me about the ROP class.

"Jordan? You still there?"

"Sure. I'm still here. Where would I go?"

"Well, after studying, maybe you'd go out for a hamburger with me. I'll have you home by seven-thirty. What do you say?"

What *do* I say? If I say, "No, I'm not interested," I lose my chance to learn more about Drew Richards. If I say, "Yes, I'd love to," I've committed myself to blood and bed pans. Why are decisions always so difficult?

"Yes, I'd love to."

                    *   *   *

As soon as I hung up, the phone rang again. It was Pam, and it was now or never. Breaking the news is never easy.

"Pam," I said. "I won't be walking home with you tomorrow. I'm going to the library. I think I'm getting a boyfriend."

There was a momentary silence on the other end. And then: "You're getting one at the library? Are they going out for loan or something? That's pretty neat. Maybe I'll go too. Does it work the same way the books do—fourteen days to return or pay the fine? If I like the cover, do I still have to read the whole boy?"

"I'm going out with Drew Richards."

"Who's he?"

"I met him in ROP."

More silence. Then, "Is it too late for me to join that class? Hey, wait a minute. You met a *boy* in nurse's training? I hate to be a chauvinist or anything like that, Jordan, but a *boy* in nurse's training? How many boys are in there, anyway? Is this some secret you've been keeping from Carrie and me? We promised to share, remember?"

"He's in nurse's training 'cause he wants to be a doctor and the other class was full. You are being sort of sexist, if I do say so myself." (I didn't bother telling her that the very same thoughts had run through my head.) "He's the *only* boy in the class. And he's already taken."

"That serious, huh?"

I was starting to dislike Pam's tone of voice. "Look, I've got to go now. My dinner is getting cold. I'll see you tomorrow at school, okay?"

"Sure, Jordan. I'll be there. If you're not too busy to talk to me, that is. You'll recognize me because I'll be hanging around a short blond girl and there'll be a big hole in the middle where Jordan Collins used to stand." Click.

"Pam . . . Pam . . ."

Now what had I done? Nothing really, only I'd done it *before* Pam. Mom's lasagna tasted like cardboard. Drew Richards was reaching in and ruining everything—even my dinner.

Chapter Five

I was supposed to meet Drew after school in front of the auditorium. The anticipation was driving me crazy. In first period, Math, I was unable to answer a question because I had left my homework at home. In English, a class I usually like, I was so busy dreaming up clever things to say to Drew, I hardly heard the teacher. In Drama I forgot my lines. And in Phys. Ed. I got hit on the head with a volleyball.

At lunch I looked for Drew but didn't see him anywhere. It's funny how you can spend two years at the same place with the same person and not know he exists, and then one day, *whammy*, finding him becomes all-important. Of course a thousand other kids were in the way, making it sort of tough.

I caught a glimpse of him between fifth and sixth periods, but when I looked again he was gone. Walking down the hall between classes is a tricky proposition. Our school is crowded, and if you try to walk against the mass of humanity, it's like trying to swim against a riptide.

Impossible. When I saw Drew I tried to make my way through the current—on the wrong side of the hall—and ended up sprawled on the floor surrounded by the flotsam from my notebook plus assorted papers and pencils. Luckily, Carrie came to my rescue.

"I've been looking for you all day," she said, helping me to my feet. "What are you doing on the floor?"

"I fell," I said. "You think I sat down here on purpose?"

She handed me my science book. "The bell's going to ring. So what's this about a boyfriend?"

I eyed her suspiciously. "Have you been tapping my phone?"

"No. Just listening to Pam."

"Pam exaggerates," I said.

"No kidding."

"Listen, I can't talk now; I'll be late for class. I'll explain later."

"*When* later?"

"Tonight later, after I have something to explain."

"I'll be holding my breath," she said, and waved good-bye.

I walked into my last class of the day. Only fifty-five more minutes to go. *I* was the one holding my breath.

* * *

I dashed into the girls' room, brushed my hair, put on some lip gloss, and straightened my skirt. Suddenly I wished I had worn pants. A skirt made it seem like I was dressing up for him, which I was, only I hated to be so obvious. Too late now. I spritzed myself with cologne, then worried that it was too strong. I scrubbed some of it off, leaving a red mark on my neck. Everything I did to make me look better ended up making me look worse!

Finally I was as ready as I could get. By the time I made my way to the auditorium, the crowds had thinned out considerably.

Drew was standing there waiting for me. "I thought I'd been stood up," he said.

I blushed. I could feel my cheeks grow hot. "I had to go to my locker, and it's on the third floor," I told him.

"No harm done. Here, let me take those." He tucked my books under his arm, right next to his. I thought I noticed his one shoulder sag some under the weight. "I have the car today," he told me.

He led the way to the car and opened the door. "You a junior?" he asked.

I nodded.

"I thought so."

"Don't hold it against me."

He laughed. Drew is a senior. After that first day in ROP class I'd rushed home and looked through my last year's yearbook until I found his picture. His being a senior made it tougher for me to find out much about him. I hardly know any seniors well, except for Tommy Tompkins—and I wasn't about to ask him.

"Did you go over any of that homework?" Drew asked me.

"I glanced at it," I said.

When Drew pulled into the library parking lot part of me was relieved and part of me disappointed. The fact that he hadn't headed directly for the hills suggested he was honest. On the other hand, maybe he was only interested in me because he thought I could help him with the class.

We found a secluded table at the back of the library and

went right to work. Drew pulled out last week's assignment. "What does *ambulate* mean?" he asked. "And how do you abbreviate that?"

"Hold on. Let me get my notes."

*   *   *

We worked all afternoon and actually made some progress. After a while I even relaxed and started to really enjoy being with Drew. I no longer cared *why* he was with me; just being with him was enough. Anyway, I knew it was only my old lack of self-confidence that had made me question his motivation.

I was looking up *pulse* and *respiration* when Drew nudged me. "I think your friends are here," he whispered.

"Where?" I asked. I looked around but didn't see anyone familiar.

"There," he said. "Behind the biographies."

Sure enough, I caught a glimpse of Pam's dark hair and heard Carrie's high-pitched giggle.

"Do they spy on you often?" he asked. He seemed amused.

"Only when I'm with a boy," I admitted.

"Is that often?" he asked.

Before I could respond, I saw the librarian heading down the aisle toward Pam and Carrie. Evidently they saw her too, because the next thing we heard was a big crash. Pam, Carrie, and the bookcart went flying. Books fell everywhere.

"Would you mind if we got out of here?" I asked, not sure whether it was anger or embarrassment I was feeling.

"No. I'm getting hungry anyway." Once again Drew

carried my books, only this time his free hand reached for mine.

I wanted to forget about my two clown friends sprawled out on the library floor, but somehow I couldn't. In all fairness, I guess curiosity would have gotten the best of me, too, if it had been Pam or Carrie with a new boy.

"You feel like hamburgers or pizza?" Drew asked.

I shrugged my shoulders. "I don't care." Actually, I wasn't hungry at all. I was too nervous to eat.

Drew ate enough for both of us, and he wasn't even embarrassed when the topping slid off his pizza and onto his plate. *I* would have died, but he just laughed, picked it up, and whisked it back onto the crust. I fiddled with my slice and worried that I had mushrooms between my teeth and tomato paste down the front of my blouse.

How do girls do this on a regular basis? I wondered. All the ones I notice with dates always look so relaxed. They flash warm golden smiles that look good enough for toothpaste advertisements. I was so uptight I felt I might break in two.

"What's the matter?" Drew asked. "Don't you like the pizza?"

"I'm on a diet," I explained.

"You don't need to be," he said.

I took a sip of Coke and choked on the ice. Please don't let me spit on him, I prayed. Please.

"You okay?" He was patting me on the back.

Finally I was able to gasp, "It went down the wrong way."

"I guess so," he said.

*   *   *

On the way home I sat closer to Drew than I had coming from school. I still wasn't totally relaxed, but I had to laugh a little when he turned on the radio and then sang to me.

"You don't like my singing?" he asked. Actually, he had a very nice voice.

"It's not that, it's just . . . well, I had this vision of you as the singing doctor. Terrific bedside manner. All of your patients would get well faster just to escape your daily lullaby."

"Very funny."

We were in front of my house. The narrow street was dark except for the porch light Mom had left on for me. I was glad the house sat back comfortably from the street.

"Well, thanks for the help," he said.

"Thank you for dinner," I told him. "I had a good time."

"So did I," he said before leaning over and kissing me very softly on the mouth. It was all so simple and so natural. It seemed funny that I had been so worried about it.

He slid out his door and was around to my side of the car before I knew what was happening. "I could have opened the door for myself," I told him.

"I *knew* you were that type. Of course you could have. But I wanted an excuse to walk you to your door."

"Do you need an excuse?" I teased.

"I hope not. And I hope you'll go out with me again." Then he kissed me again, only this time his arms went around me. It felt good to be held by Drew. "Good night, Jordan."

"Good night." I turned around and opened the door and prayed that my family was at the other end of the house. This moment was too special to share with them. I wanted to keep the memory of Drew's kiss all to myself.

*   *   *

"I guess you didn't have onions on your pizza then, did you?" Carrie was on the phone, grilling me about my date.

"What were you two doing hiding behind the biographies?" I asked her. "I was so embarrassed. Even Drew saw you."

"We saw him too, Jordan. He's cute. Well, actually, we were hanging around the philosophy section where we had a really great view, only Pam said she needed a biography for English so we decided to kill two birds with one stone, so to speak."

"It looked to me like you almost killed yourselves."

"Oh, that. Mrs. Kingsley made us pick every book up off the floor and *then* she made us shelve them. We were there until six o'clock. She should have been a jail warden, not a librarian. Are you going out with him again?" she asked. "Pam is so jealous, you should see her. I'm not jealous, Jordan, honest. I'm happy for you. Does he have a brother or a cousin?"

"I don't know. I'll ask."

"Couldn't you just call Pam and tell her it's not that big a deal? She seems to be feeling really left out or betrayed or something. I think she's worried she'll be an old maid, just when values are changing and getting married is starting to be 'in' again."

"Oh, for heaven's sake. I've never heard of a sixteen-year-old old maid."

"Well, I haven't either, but according to Pam, it's a

state of mind that has nothing to do with age.''

I said good-bye to Carrie and went into the bathroom to get ready for bed. I smiled at myself in the mirror. Amazing. There wasn't even a trace of mushroom between my teeth. And my mouth didn't look crooked. I realized there was no longer any need to consult with Julius about my kissing technique. I guess I kiss okay. If not, I'm sure Drew would have told me.

By the way, Jordan, I like you a lot, but your kiss is crooked.

Suddenly a thought occurred to me. Maybe Drew kissed crooked too. How would I know? I guess as long as we're both crooked the same way it doesn't really matter.

Thank goodness I don't wear braces. I don't need any more complications in my life.

Chapter Six

The next day at school Pam was cool and distant. I didn't know what to do about it, so I did nothing. Carrie chattered on incessantly. "Come on, let's find Drew," she said. "I want to get a look at him close up. What's his schedule?"

"I don't know," I told her truthfully.

"How can you not know?" she asked me, astonished. "That's the first step in getting to know a guy. How are you ever going to bump into him accidentally if you don't know *where* he'll be and *when* he'll be there?"

"I guess I didn't follow directions," I said.

"I should say you didn't. It's amazing you've gotten this far. What lunch does he have?"

"I don't know," I had to admit.

"You don't know that either? Do you realize you're completely at his mercy? He could sneak up on you at any time. You won't be prepared with any of the proper comebacks."

"Why do I need a comeback?" I asked.

31

"Oh, for goodness' sake," Carrie said, disgusted.

"I'll see you guys later, okay?" Pam took off across the parking lot before I could protest.

"I don't think Pam likes all this boy-talk, Carrie."

"Oh, she'll get over it," Carrie said. "She's still mooning over Pomerantz, but he was all wrong for her. They're exactly the same height."

"What does that have to do with anything?"

"You can't date a boy who's the same size as you! That means you'd have to wear flats to all the dances or risk towering over him."

"Carrie, I think your sense of what's important is really screwed up."

"Oh yeah? Well, you just check out Ronnie Davis and Carol Petie the next time they walk by. I bet he either stands on a big rock or she stands in a trench in order to kiss. Imagine how uncomfortable that is. And they're really serious. Would you want to spend the rest of your life looking around for a trench or a boulder every time you wanted to kiss?"

I had to laugh at Carrie. She thinks of the silliest things.

"Is Drew taller than you?"

"Yes."

"Good. You did one thing right. When are you two going out again?"

"I don't know."

"You mean you let him get away without a definite commitment?"

"Well, I'll see him in class on Saturday."

"Yeah, but that's not a date."

"I'm not sure I want to date, Carrie. It's too confusing."

"Nonsense. It's just a matter of memorizing a few basics."

"Like what?"

Carrie looked at me and shook her head. "Oh, for goodness' sake," she said.

Just then the bell rang, and I walked to class wondering what basics I hadn't memorized. Carrie reads all the girls' magazines, so I imagine she's pretty well prepared for any contingency that comes her way. As far as I can tell, *no* contingencies have come her way yet, which might be why she's so eager to tell me what to do, sort of dating by osmosis.

I was deep in thought pondering all this when I accidentally bumped into Drew. The thought occurred to me that perhaps he'd "accidentally" bumped into me, but I immediately dismissed it.

"Hi," he said.

"Hi," I said.

"Where you off to?"

"Phys. Ed. to get hit on the head with a volleyball. How 'bout you?"

"Calculus."

"Yuck."

"Yeah, that's what I say."

Calculus. Fourth period. Carrie would be proud of me. Drew looked as though he too was making mental notes: Phys. Ed. Fourth period. No, I was probably imagining it.

"I hear Tucker's really hard for Calculus," I said. (Clever, clever.)

"I guess so, but I have Mathieson," he told me. "He's okay."

Mathieson. Calculus. Fourth period. I committed it to memory.

The second bell rang. "You'll be late," he said.

"Yeah. You too."

"Well, see ya."

"Yeah, see ya."

I was getting the hang of this. Now all I needed to do was find out what room Mathieson had for fourth period.

*   *   *

"He has Mathieson fourth period for Calculus," I told Carrie. Pam had gone home early with a headache, so it was just Carrie and me on the walk home.

"Good. You're catching on," she said. "Only five more periods and you'll have his entire schedule. How did you get Mathieson?"

"I asked him."

"You *asked* him?" she said, horrified. "You can't do that."

"Why not?"

"Because you just can't, that's why. It isn't done. You have to be sneaky and underhanded. It's more fun that way."

"Why do I have to sneak when he'll tell me if I just ask him?"

Carrie threw up her hands in disgust. "Oh, for goodness' sake," she said.

*   *   *

For the rest of the week I saw Drew every day in the hall between third and fourth periods. It didn't give us much time to talk. I did learn, however, that he worked after school three days a week at Richard's Automotive Shop.

"That's bad," Carrie said.

"Why is that bad?" I asked her.

Her blue eyes flashed at me. "It's the worst possible place he could work. There's no way you can fake it."

I looked at her questioningly. "Fake what?"

"Look," she said matter-of-factly. "If he worked at a fast-food joint, you could fake hunger or thirst in order to see him. If he worked in a clothing store, you could pretend you needed to buy something for your father's birthday. But you can't exactly pretend you need a new spark plug or engine—he'd never go for that!"

Carrie had a point.

"I'll have to think about this," she said. "There's got to be some way around it. What days does he work?"

"I don't know."

Carrie thought for a moment and then said, "Well, we know he doesn't work Fridays because you went to that first class on Friday, right?"

"Right," I said.

"What day did we go to the library?"

"Monday."

"So, just for the sake of argument, let's assume he works Tuesdays, Wednesdays, and Thursdays."

"Why are we going to argue?"

"We're not. We're going to break down in front of the auto shop."

"Carrie," I said. "We're going to argue. I'm not breaking down anywhere. I don't even get my license for another few weeks."

"Well, *I'll* break down then," she said. "You'll just have to be with me."

I could see her wheels turning, hatching a fantastic plot.

"Oh, for goodness' sake," I mimicked.

*   *   *

Ten o'clock Saturday morning I found myself sitting in room 210 waiting for Miss Piaget. I had my homework, my notebook, and my lunch in hand. Drew walked in two minutes later and sat down right behind me. I felt uncomfortable knowing he was staring at my back. Did my hair look clean? Did I have ring-around-the-collar? Did my tuna-fish sandwich smell? Was I slouching?

I sat up straight and tried to listen to Miss Piaget. She was going too fast. I can't think about more than one thing at a time, and right then I was thinking about Drew. Next Saturday I would choose a seat in the very back. It was safer.

She was handing out our assignments. "Each of you will be assigned to a specific section of the hospital where you will be expected to perform those duties we have discussed in class. You will be working under a nurse on duty who will report back to me in writing on how well you carried out your responsibilities."

For the rest of the hour we went over equipment and supplies. I learned how to make a bed, I learned the bed positions, and I learned where I could find the footboards, cradles, donuts, and sheepskins needed in hospital work.

Before I knew it, we were being loaded onto the bus. Drew sat down next to me. I was starving, but I didn't want to eat my tuna fish in front of him.

"What do you have?" he asked, opening his lunch.

"Tuna."

"I have egg salad."

Egg salad struck me as equally gross, so I went ahead and ate, washing it all down with apple juice.

Drew pulled out his assignment slip. "I have pediatrics. How about you?"

"Geriatrics. That's old people, right?"

"Right."

"Well, I like old people," I said. "I love my grandpa."

"Sick old people can be kind of crochety," he said. "But I guess they aren't any worse than cranky little kids. I was sort of hoping for post-op, though."

The bus pulled into the West Valley Hospital parking lot. It was the same hospital we always came to for emergencies. Twice Jimmy had been here for asthma attacks, and we once had to bring Jessica here when she fell out of a tree and dislocated her shoulder. So far, I'd had no need for a hurried visit here.

We were escorted through the back service entrance and down the stairs to a classroom. The basement was poorly lit and had a weird smell to it, sort of a combination of floor wax, antiseptic, and alcohol.

We passed the cafeteria and the engineering room. A sign on the wall indicated that the morgue was to the left. Drew nudged me and whispered, "I guess the food must be pretty bad and that's why they put both places on the same floor."

"Remind me not to eat here," I whispered back.

We lined up according to our assignments. Miss Piaget gave us some last-minute instructions, and then each small group followed an orderly for a general tour of the hospital.

Just my luck to get stuck with Otto. Otto reminded me of one of the bad guys in a James Bond movie. I didn't like the way he kept looking at me.

"You're gonna like it here," he said. He held open the door to the service elevator, and the geriatrics group stepped in. The doors closed quickly, and I felt like Otto's captive. I glanced at the three other girls with me. They didn't look particularly worried.

The elevator lurched and came to a stop between floors. Otto banged on the service panel. Several buttons lit up and then the machinery groaned and reluctantly moved on again.

"This elevator sticks sometimes," he said. I couldn't stop staring at Otto's large bald head. "Geriatrics is on the fifth floor," he explained.

"Where's pediatrics?" I asked cheerfully.

"Fourth floor, but we're not going there."

"Thank you very much."

The doors swung back with a creak, and we exited on the fifth floor. "This is it, girls," he said. "Sign in here and then we'll finish our tour of the floor. You need to know where the supplies are, where the food service comes up, and a few million other things. And we haven't got all day." Otto grinned at us again. I was surprised to see he had all his teeth and that they looked normal. I was fully expecting pointed metal ones, and I doubted very seriously that James Bond would ever think to look for me here on the fifth-floor geriatrics ward.

Chapter Seven

Over the course of the next few weeks I learned a lot about nursing. Mostly nursing is just plain hard work. I think it takes a caring, concerned, loving person to be a nurse, and I'm not sure I came equipped with the proper qualifications. But I'm trying my best.

One of the things they keep hammering at us over and over again is that a patient is much more than a physical ailment. I guess because a hospital is a place where people work to fix the physical problem, there's a tendency to forget about the emotional aspects of illness. But we are taught that a patient's feelings have a lot to do with his recovery.

For instance, we've been warned never to refer to the patients as "the broken leg in room five-oh-three," or "Grandpa in bed ten." But one of my favorite "Grandpas" is Mr. Harris in geriatrics.

Mr. Harris is a seventy-six-year-old ex-high school history teacher. He had a stroke and he hardly speaks at all except to swear at people. His only remaining family is his daughter, and she hardly comes to visit him because his language embarrasses her. It doesn't embarrass me, though. I've heard worse. When you live with two fighting ten-year-olds, you're bound to hear it all. The nurses say Mr. Harris is senile, but I don't think he is. That's not my diagnosis or anything because we're not supposed to diagnose; I just don't believe it.

Mr. Harris likes to go to the sun room, so I take him there every chance I get. It's light and airy and cheery in there, and you can see out over the whole city. Mr. Harris understands everything I say to him. I know he does.

Sometimes I even come to visit him after school. I read to him. He likes Kipling a lot, especially "Gunga Din." When I'm finished reading, he says, "Damn good . . . damn good," over and over again.

I hardly ever see Drew on Saturday afternoons. They really keep us busy. One Saturday, though, I was supposed to replace the tissues in each room. Before I was finished, I ran out, so she sent me down to the fourth-floor supply room for more. The first thing I saw when I got off the elevator was Drew wheeling a pretty girl up and down the hall. She didn't look very sick to me, and she didn't look like any toddler.

I couldn't help passing them, so I said hi.

"Hi," he answered. I thought he looked embarrassed.

Why was *he* embarrassed? I was the one rolling a cart full of tissues and toilet paper.

"Jordan," he said, "this is Susie."

"Hi, Susie," I said and tried my best to give her a big smile. Susie has short dark hair cut like a pixie's and big brown eyes. Her entire face was swallowed up in those liquid pools. I worried about Drew drowning in them, but then I remembered he was just doing his job.

Was she studying me more closely than necessary? "Well," I told them, "it's back to the fifth floor. See ya."

I rolled my cart onto the service elevator and waited until the doors banged shut. As usual, it lurched and chugged upward, complaining all the way. I don't like elevators in general, but I especially hate this one. It scares me. I've decided that if and when it goes, I'll save myself by jumping up at the last moment. Of course it will be real tricky knowing exactly when the last moment *is*. Dad once explained to me that according to some physics principle, my plan will never work, but still I'm going to give it a try if I'm ever in an elevator and the cable breaks.

As I got off the elevator, Otto was wheeling a patient on. He smiled at me, but for some reason his smile always seems more like a leer.

Later I asked one of the other girls, Chris, if she noticed anything strange about Otto.

"Otto?" she said, astonished. "Otto's real nice, Jordan. Honest. He's taught me a lot."

I don't want Otto teaching me anything, so I think I'll try to stay out of his way.

*   *   *

I still saw Drew in the halls between third and fourth periods, but he didn't ask me out again. I told myself he didn't have time to ask me out. The halls were crowded and noisy; half the time I couldn't hear what he said, so I just smiled and nodded. He probably thought I was a real yo-yo.

"He could ask you out if he wanted to," Carrie said. (She's wonderful for my self-confidence.)

"It's crowded and noisy in the halls, and he doesn't have time," I told her.

"Oh yeah?" she said skeptically. "Experiment time." We were walking together to Spanish. She held up her watch and shouted at the top of her lungs, "Would you go out with me Saturday night, Jordan?"

It seemed as though the entire student body turned around to stare at us. Some giggled. Carrie ignored them. "That took exactly four seconds to say, Jordan. Giving him a little leeway for nervousness and being tongue-tied, he'd still have plenty of time to ask you out. You've obviously done something wrong."

"Thanks a lot."

"Not to worry. We'll fix it."

*   *   *

On Thursday afternoon Carrie and I planned a shopping excursion to the mall. Carrie borrowed her mom's car so we could leave right after school. Pam didn't want to go with us; I think she's still waiting for her hair to grow.

"I'm going to buy a new pair of jeans and maybe a new blouse if I can find one," Carrie told me. "How about you?"

"I think I'll just look around," I said. "Of course, if I see something special . . ."

Carrie drove down the street and turned right. "Hey, you're going the wrong way," I said. "I thought we were going to the new mall. You need to take the Interstate back the other way."

Carrie kept driving. "Carrie! Turn around. We're headed toward town."

"I know. I have to get something first. Do you mind?"

I looked at my watch. "I guess not, but I have to be home by six. This sort of cuts into our shopping time."

Carrie drove and hummed to herself. "What are you buying?" I asked.

"I'm buying you a second chance," she said. At first I didn't know what she was talking about, and then . . . well, by then it was too late.

She stopped in the middle of the street. Cars honked. "Carrie, what are you doing?" She jumped out of the car and lifted the hood.

"What's wrong?" I asked, leaning out of the car.

"Severed fan belt," she said. "Or it will be if I can ever sever it."

More cars honked. I was getting nervous. I looked around anxiously, hoping for help from somewhere. "What do you mean, if you can sever it?"

"Got it!" I heard her exclaim.

"Carrie. Carrie, where are you going? Don't leave me here. Oh, no!"

Carrie left me stranded in the middle of the street while she hurried to complete her plan. I didn't have to watch her. I knew. Richard's Automotive Shop was her destination.

I hunched down in my seat. Maybe I would get lucky and some maniac driver hauling down Sixth Street would put an instant end to my misery.

No such luck. They all went politely around. I crouched lower but peeked occasionally out the window. What I saw made me wish for instant invisibility.

"Jordan," Drew said. "What are you doing on the floor?"

"Tying my shoe."

"Tying your shoe?"

"Yeah. Both of them."

"Well, hurry up and tie and get behind the wheel. I'm going to push you into our driveway."

I did as I was told. I had no choice. As I steered, I caught sight of Carrie standing on the sidewalk, cheerfully waving the severed fan belt at me.

It took about twenty minutes for Drew to finish writing up another customer's order, then locate the correct size fan belt and install it. Carrie chatted on non-stop. "Funny how those things wear out. And my dad usually takes such care of his vehicles."

Drew inspected the broken belt. "It doesn't look worn to me," he said. "It looks like something cut it in two. What a nice coincidence it happened right here."

I went over to the gum machine and kept putting my money in. Green, pink, black gumballs were my reward. I felt like stuffing them down Carrie's throat.

She paid for the fan belt, and then we were on our way again. I was so angry with her I was afraid to speak.

Finally, Carrie broke the silence. "Did he say anything to you?" she asked.

"Nothing that justified what you just did."

"Oh. I thought maybe he'd ask you out."

"Well, he didn't."

"Too bad. That fan belt cost more than I figured it would."

"Too bad."

"Well, I tried."

"You *tried?* You tried humiliating me, embarrassing me, making a fool of me! I wanted to die, Carrie. Right there on the spot. It was the worst moment of my entire life, and I don't think I'm ever going to speak to you again!"

Big tears formed in her eyes and threatened to spill down her cheeks. That made me feel worse than ever. But I wasn't about to forgive her.

* * *

That night Drew called, so I guess Carrie's plan worked. But she sure put me in an awkward position.

"Hi," he said.

"Hi," I said.

"It sure was funny how that fan belt just happened to break right in front of the auto shop, don't you think?"

"Hysterical," I said.

"Does your friend's car often break down like that?"

"Only at inopportune moments," I answered him.

"Well, it wasn't too inopportune for me," Drew said. "I sort of enjoyed it."

"You did?"

"Sure. It gave me a chance to see you."

"Oh."

"Your friend's car isn't too predictable, I guess."

"Nothing about Carrie is too predictable," I said.

"Well, it was just lucky that you got stuck where you did. Say, would you like to go to the movies with me?"

"Sure," I said. "When?"

"Next Friday night?"

"Great," I told him.

"Well, see ya."

"Yeah. See ya."

He hung up. I listened until I was sure the line was dead and then I did my Indian war-whoop around my room. I knew I should call and thank Carrie, but I decided to let her pay for her prank a little longer. I hung the severed fan belt on my bulletin board, and every time I looked at it I just had to smile.

Chapter Eight

You'd think I'd learn, but no, dumb Jordan made the fatal mistake of telling Carrie that Drew had invited me to the movies. If I'd been thinking rationally—if I'd been thinking at *all*—I would have realized how foolish that was. Never underestimate a crazy friend.

He picked me up at six forty-five. I changed my clothes about eight million times, but finally settled on brown slacks and a sweater. I didn't look beautiful, but I've decided neat is what I should strive for. Neat is attainable.

Dad grilled Drew about what movie we were going to and what time we'd be back. Jessica and Jimmy just stood and stared as if they'd never seen a boy before. (Well, in all fairness, they'd never seen one standing in our living room waiting to take me out.) I was glad when we finally said our good-byes and escaped to the safety of his car.

The movie we were going to see was a sad, romantic one about two teenagers who fall in love. It gave me sort of a shivery feeling to know that Drew had picked out a love story.

For some reason, romance and Jordan Collins just don't seem to go together. To begin with, when we entered the theater, the credits were already rolling, which meant that it was pretty dark and we could hardly see where we were going. I almost sat in some sailor's lap. And when I did find an empty seat, I sat down on this kid's wad of bubble gum.

As I was trying to scrape the mess off my slacks without attracting Drew's attention, I thought I heard a familiar giggle behind me. Please don't let that be Carrie, I prayed silently: Please make her be safe and sound at home watching TV. When a piece of popcorn hit me on the side of the head, I knew my prayer was in vain.

How was I supposed to concentrate on the movie with Carrie and Pam behind me, watching Drew's every move? He put his arm around me and I heard giggles. He leaned over and whispered something in my ear, which I didn't hear because I was so nervous about my friends the spies. More giggles. What were they doing?

When the movie ended and we got up to leave, another embarrassing thing happened. Half the audience was still crying over the sad ending, yours truly included. More embarrassment, sniffling in front of Drew. But the worst was yet to come: half-blinded by my tears, I immediately stepped into a Coke cup and got it stuck on my foot.

I tried kicking it off. No luck. I tried hopping it off. No luck. I tried walking it off. Finally I had to bend down and pull it off my shoe. The people behind us witnessed this little scenario and some of them found it funny enough to chuckle over. (I would guess I've been to the movies at least a hundred times in my life, and not once have I ever seen anyone else get a foot stuck inside a cup.)

"Aren't those your friends over there?" Drew asked.

"Where?"

"Over there," he said, pointing. "Standing next to the snack bar."

"What a coincidence," I said bleakly.

"Want to say hi?" he asked.

"No thanks," I answered, tying my coat around my waist in an effort to hide the gum that was still stuck to my bottom. "I'll probably talk to them tomorrow anyway."

And when I do . . .

*   *   *

Drew kissed me good night at the door. Actually, he kissed me several times. Actually, I kissed him back, although I couldn't quite figure out why he'd want to kiss someone with gum on her fanny, popcorn in her hair, and Coca-Cola on her shoe. Maybe he's deficient in something, like iron deficiency anemia. Maybe kissing rejuvenates him or something. Maybe he didn't know about the gum and the popcorn.

Maybe . . . maybe he likes me?

*   *   *

"What were you doing spying on me, Carrie? That was absolutely the grossest thing you've ever done," I yelled at her through the receiver.

"Gosh, Jordan, Pam and I were planning on seeing that movie anyway, and well, well . . . I was just concerned that you were dating a nice person. You know, someone who would be polite and treat you right and . . ."

"*And?*" I demanded.

"And he seems to be a nice person," she said meekly.

"And what if he wasn't? What would you have done about it? Would you have sat on him, hit him, caused a big scene just to save your friend?''

There was a long pause. "Maybe," she said finally.

"*Maybe?*" I asked, incredulous. I should have known better.

"Not maybe. Yes. A definite yes. But isn't it nice to know that someone has your best interests at heart?''

*   *   *

I guess Pam's hair has grown sufficiently or else she's forgiven me for starting to date because she's speaking to me again. Probably the real truth of the matter is she's hoping for a few tips, a few pointers from me for when she starts going out.

Not that I have any, except maybe to watch where you're stepping. What else could I say? This is all pretty new to me, too.

Dating, and keeping up with my classes and hospital work is all taking up a lot of my time. And I still like to get in to see Mr. Harris as often as I can.

Thursday after school, Pam's mom gave me a ride to the hospital, which is right on the way to Pam's flute lesson. I stuffed my books in my locker, put my apron on, and took the elevator directly to the fifth floor.

Mr. Harris seemed much improved. So much so that I got permission to wheel him around outside on the grounds. I put a blanket around his knees and grabbed an extra one for his shoulders in case it turned out to be too cool for him outside.

West Valley Hospital has a garden area that is well maintained by several garden clubs in town. Different flowers are almost always blooming, at least in the spring. I wheeled Mr. Harris down to smell them.

He seemed to like being outside, so I decided to give

him a tour of the grounds. We were rounding the corner of the building when we ran smack into Drew and Susie Big-eyes. I was glad Mr. Harris's wheelchair came equipped with a safety belt.

I guess Drew likes to get in to see his patient, too. "Hello," he said.

"Hello," I said. I know it sounded unfriendly. "Well, excuse us," I managed. "It's time for Mr. Harris to get back upstairs." I swung Mr. Harris's wheelchair around and headed for the doors.

"Jordan, wait!" Drew ran after us. "What's the matter with you?"

"What's the matter?" I said. "Nothing's the matter. You left your patient all alone, Drew. Rule number one: never leave your patient unattended."

"Ah, I get it," he said.

"Get what?" I retorted.

"It's Susie, isn't it? You're jealous."

"You're crazy. Don't be ridiculous."

"You're the one who's being ridiculous."

I turned to face him squarely. "*That*," I said, pointing to Susie, "is *not* a toddler. You told me you were working in pediatrics, as in little people, babies, children—you know, wet diapers, snotty noses." I grabbed the handles of Mr. Harris's chair and wheeled him toward the door. He was reciting to himself. "It was Din, Din, Din," he exclaimed.

Drew grabbed the chair and stopped us. "If you had been paying any attention in class, Jordan, you would have heard that pediatrics goes up to age sixteen. Susie is sixteen." We both looked over at her. She smiled back at us.

"It's just that I thought . . . that we were, I mean . . ." I was stammering all over the place.

"You're a better man than I am Gunga Din!" Mr. Harris shouted with enthusiasm.

"You thought we were dating. We are," he said. "And it has nothing to do with Susie. I try to spend time with her because she's sort of lonely here. Most of the other kids on the ward are much younger than her."

Now I felt crummy. "What's wrong with her?" I whispered.

"Some sort of blood disease. They keep trying new medications, hoping one will take hold. That's why she has to stay here, so they can monitor the effects of the drugs."

"I'm sorry," I said. "Sorry for thinking . . ."

"For thinking the worst? Why? I sort of like it when you're jealous. It makes your eyes sparkle."

"It was Din, Din, Din," Mr. Harris yelled again.

"I'd better get him back upstairs," I said.

"I'll call you tonight," Drew told me. He leaned over and kissed me softly on the forehead.

"Okay." I watched him walk back to Susie. I waved to her once more. I blinked back the tears, but I couldn't seem to swallow the big lump in my throat. Somewhere along the line I was going to have to stop acting like such a jerk.

"It was Din, Din, Din . . ."

Chapter Nine

I think I've changed my mind about being a doctor. There're some good things about it, sure, but there're some real crummy things, too. Some people don't get well again. Some people are in pain and there's nothing anyone can do about it. Some diseases disfigure; some medications have terrible side effects.

After working in the hospital, I will never again complain about how I look. I look okay. My body may not be beautiful, but at least everything is there and it all works. I guess I've been a crybaby—a real jerk.

"Hospital work certainly has taught you compassion," Mom said after I told her about some of the things I'd seen on the ward. "I'm glad you realize just how lucky you are, Jordan." She kissed me on the head and poured herself a cup of tea. "I guess Dad and I have tried to protect you kids from some of the more unpleasant facts of life. Maybe we were wrong to try. I don't know," she said. She sat down on the stool in the kitchen. "Help me think of something new and exciting for dinner," she said.

"I can't." I told her. "I'm not very hungry."

"You know, Jordan, just because you're exposed to some unpleasant realities doesn't mean you have to be depressed all the time. If anything, you should strive to make each day as pleasant and as wonderful as possible. Your contact with the hospital should only increase your appreciation of the truly beautiful things in life." Mom stared hard at me. "Do I sound like a Pollyanna?" she asked.

"Sort of."

She nodded and took a sip of tea. "Just think about it," she said.

That's what I like about Mom. She never tries to make decisions for me. Mostly she just presents the facts, along with her opinion, and then backs off to give me time to make up my own mind.

My own mind was made up. I'd stay with the program because I was in too deep to quit. I could use the extra credits. Besides, I like Mr. Harris and of course I like being with Drew, even if we are only together in class for an hour. So I don't have the makings of a Marcus Welby or even a Florence Nightingale. I might as well stick with it, learn a little and maybe help a lot.

I already know how to save a person from choking. I know mouth-to-mouth resuscitation. I know how to do C.P.R., although I'm not sure I wouldn't forget everything if I ever had to do it for real.

We practiced on a dummy named Matilda. The breathing technique was pretty embarrassing because most of the girls in class knew I was going out with Drew. So when it was his turn with Matilda, the comments really flew.

"Nice he can practice on a dummy," Chris said.

"Matilda or Jordan?" Wendy teased.

Even I chuckled, but I wondered how funny they'd think it was if they knew I had once practiced kissing with Julius, my stuffed elephant.

*   *   *

Everyone at school is talking about the Spring Dance, especially Carrie and Pam, who are doing their best to find dates.

"I saw the perfect dress in the window of Broadway," Pam said. "It will look super on me. I know I can convince my mom to buy it for me."

"First you have to convince some boy to invite you," Carrie said.

"Don't worry. I'm working on it," Pam said with a definite twinkle in her eye. "What about you, Jordan? Has Drew said anything about the dance yet?"

"Not yet," I told her.

"Well, he will. It's still early."

"I hope so."

"Wouldn't it be fun if we could all go together?" Pam said. "I can't wait to get that dress. What are you two going to wear?"

"Aren't you being just a bit premature?" Carrie asked her.

"I'm planning ahead, that's all. And if I don't go to this dance, at least I'll have the dress to wear to the next one. Someday, *someone* has to ask me."

"Wanna bet?" Carrie said, grinning devilishly.

Pam tried to swat Carrie with her history book, but she missed. Carrie took off, running and laughing down the street.

*   *   *

My birthday this year fell on Thursday. Mom and Dad took me out to dinner. It's sort of a tradition in our family. Each year I get to pick the restaurant I want to go to. The twins get to pick on their birthday, too, only I'm the lucky one because they have to go together while on my birthday it's just Mom and Dad and me.

We went to the Seafood Cellar because I absolutely adore their beer-batter shrimp. The twins always choose Cisco's because they love Mexican food.

I was eating my salad when Mom pulled a small package out of her purse. "Here," she said, "for our birthday girl." Carefully I opened the box. Inside was a gold bracelet with my name engraved on it.

"It's really pretty," I said. "Thank you both."

Dad helped me put it around my wrist. "I guess we don't have to worry about you being sweet sixteen and never been kissed," he said.

I know I blushed like crazy, but the candlelight in the restaurant helped disguise it.

Mom knew I was embarrassed, so she said, "Dad's just teasing you, honey. You know we're both fond of your beau."

"Isn't that term just a wee bit old-fashioned," Dad said, "even for ancient fogies like us? What Mom is trying to say, Jordan, is that we both like Drew. He seems to be a very nice boy."

I leaned over and kissed them both, thanking them again for my gift. Then our dinners came.

For dessert, the waiter brought out a cake with sixteen candles on it and all the waiters sang "Happy Birthday" to me. It was embarrassing and fun at the same time. That night I went to bed stuffed and happy.

*   *   *

Friday after school Drew called and asked if he could come over. I was sort of surprised because we hadn't planned anything.

"Sure," I said. "I'll make some hot chocolate and maybe we can find a good movie on TV."

"I'll make the hot chocolate," Drew said when he got here. "I'm an expert."

"Oh yeah? I bet my hot chocolate is better than yours."

"The bet is on. The twins can be the judges."

We went to work concocting our drinks. Drew bent over his pan like he was creating something that was going to win the Nobel prize. "No fair peeking," he said.

"I'd never stoop so low," I told him. When we were ready, we poured our respective hot chocolates into mugs for the twins, reserving some for ourselves.

"Okay, kids," Drew told them. "Pick the better of the two."

Jimmy scrunched up his face and blew into one mug. He tasted it. Then he blew into the other and tried it. Jessica did the same only a little less theatrically.

"Well?" Drew asked.

"I can't tell the difference," Jimmy said.

"Me neither," Jessica mimicked.

"So much for your expert hot chocolate," I told him.

We checked the TV listings in the newspaper, but there was nothing interesting on. There never is on Friday nights.

"You kids want to play cards or something?" Drew asked the twins.

"Monopoly," Jimmy shouted, and ran to get the game.

"Now you've done it," I said. "We'll never be free of them."

Jimmy and Jessica set up the Monopoly board and then proceeded to argue about who got to use the car token.

Drew suggested they work it out while he and I danced to some records in the living room. We danced one dance and then were interrupted by the twins who kept running in and out, giggling all the time.

"The twins are cute," Drew said as he twirled me in his arms.

"Well, they sure like you," I said truthfully.

"We've worked it out!" Jessica shouted. "I'm going to be the dog and jerky Jimmy can be the car. What do you want to be, Drew?"

Fortunately, Mom and Dad came to the rescue. I heard Dad tell the twins that he would play Monopoly with them. I knew he and Mom were doing it for my sake, because Dad is completely Monopolied out. (Thank you very much, Mom and Dad.)

Drew and I played gin rummy for a while. I kept winning, but it didn't seem to bother Drew. I guess he has enough self-confidence to handle that sort of thing.

At ten-thirty Drew had to leave. He said good night to my mom and dad and then said to me, "Could you walk out to the car with me, Jordan?" Suddenly he seemed sort of shy. "I have a surprise for you," he said.

We tiptoed out the front door and down the walk. I guess Mom had put the twins to bed because they didn't follow us. I kept expecting them to grab us or jump out from behind the closest bush. But we really were alone.

Curiosity got the better of me. "A surprise? What for?"

"Close your eyes," he commanded.

I did as I was told, shivering a little, more from anticipation than from the night air. I could hear him opening the glove compartment.

"Keep your eyes closed," he said again.

"They are," I told him.

"Okay. Open them."

In the dim light from the porch I could see a small package in Drew's hand. He held it out.

"For me?" I asked.

"Yes. For your birthday."

"How did you know it was my birthday?"

"I called you last night and Jimmy said you were out celebrating."

"That stinker."

"No. I'm glad he did."

"You shouldn't have, Drew."

"I wanted to. Go ahead. Open it."

I carefully unwrapped the package, gently refolding the paper afterward.

"A paper saver, I see. My mother does the same thing."

I wondered if his mother still had the wrapping from her first gift from a boy. I knew I would save mine forever.

I opened the box. Inside, resting on a square of white cotton, was a necklace. A single pearl sat at the base of a tiny gold heart.

"Oh," I said. "It's beautiful. You shouldn't have."

"I wanted to, Jordan. Here, put it on." Drew lifted the necklace out of the box and fastened the clasp around my neck.

"I don't know what to say. Thank you."

He put his arms around me and pulled me toward him. "You don't have to say anything. In fact, the less talking, the better."

His warm lips met mine, and this time I shivered not from anticipation or cold, but from sheer happiness.

*　　*　　*

I wore the necklace all the time, only taking it off to

shower. Carrie and Pam were visibly impressed.

"Wow!" Carrie said. "It's beautiful."

Pam fingered it, too. "Yeah, it's great," she said. "It would look really great with my new dress," she teased.

"You got it?" I asked.

"Not only got it," she announced proudly, "but I got an invitation too. From none other than Don Pomerantz."

"No kidding. What happened to Hillary?"

"I think she spent too much time with her pompoms. And guess what else?" Pam bubbled excitedly. "Not only am *I* going, but I sort of hinted around and Don is going to ask his cousin Willy to double with Carrie. Isn't that neat? We'll all be there together."

"I don't know about me," I said slowly. "Drew hasn't said anything yet. He might not have any money. I'm sure buying the necklace cost him a lot."

"Oh, he'll ask you," Carrie said. "And you could offer to pay for the tickets. You can't miss the Spring Dance."

"I'm sure he'll ask you soon," Pam agreed.

"Maybe," I told them. I reached up and touched my necklace. Its light weight felt reassuring around my neck.

Chapter Ten

Drew started walking me to my classes as often as he could. I finally learned his schedule, not by using Carrie's methods but simply by asking him. We even started sharing lockers; his is on the basement floor of the old building, and mine is on the third floor of the new building. It makes things simpler. When I go to science on the first floor, I use his locker. When he goes to French on the third floor, he uses mine.

I guess people have started thinking of us as a couple. It's amazing how quickly your friends adjust. When I wait in line at lunch, no one ever says anything when Drew cuts in line to stand beside me. When we gather in the auditorium for assembly, kids automatically leave an extra seat next to me for Drew. It's kind of a neat feeling being one half of a couple.

He holds my hand in the halls. He carries my books. He takes me home after school whenever he has the car. He also gives Carrie and Pam a ride, which is nice.

My family is used to seeing Drew around the house.

Sometimes, on days when he doesn't have to work and we study together, he even stays for dinner. Mom seems to like him, I guess because he's so polite and helps with the dishes. And Dad's happy to have another male to discuss sports with. Jimmy likes him because Drew plays catch. And Jessica adores him because, well, because he's older.

I think even Carrie and Pam like him, only I try not to spend too much time with all of them together. I love my friends—it's not that. It's just that I'm sort of afraid Carrie will pull some crazy stunt. She's still rather unpredictable.

Having a boyfriend hasn't hurt my popularity ratings at school either. After Drew and I started going to parties, kids I knew only vaguely were suddenly eager for the pleasure of my company—or was it Drew's company?

Part of me, the cynical part, objects to this newfound social-status thing. I mean, I'm not a changed person. I'm the same old Jordan. It's almost like I didn't count until I had a boyfriend. Jordan and Drew, okay together, a big zero when bisected.

But there's another part of me that enjoys the parties, so I'm sort of stuck. Stuck between telling all these kids off, and stuck maybe not being invited anywhere again in my life. A real quandary.

*   *   *

Practically everyone is talking about and preparing for the dance. Still no invitation from Drew. I've decided we're not going. He would have said something by now. Well, it's no big thing. I still have next year.

I guess I've been moping around the house because Mom asked me about it. "Oh, everyone's going to the Spring Dance," I explained, "and Drew hasn't even mentioned it."

"Why don't *you* mention it?" she said.

"I couldn't do that."

"Why not? Your father probably wouldn't be your father, my dear, if I hadn't asked *him* to the Backwards Dance."

"That was different, Mom. That was fifty years ago."

"I beg your pardon." Her eyebrows rose and almost met in the middle.

"Well, maybe not fifty, but a long time ago."

"All the more reason for you to go ahead and talk to Drew. Things are more flexible now. Girls have more options. You're never going to get what you want, Jordan, unless you go after it." She put the finishing touches on a chocolate cake and handed me the bowl. I stuck one finger in and swirled it around in the remaining frosting.

"Why don't you offer to pay for the tickets?" Mom went on. "Maybe Drew has some financial obligation you're not aware of, and can't afford to go."

"Maybe," I said. I licked the spatula clean and put it in the sink. "But somehow, I don't think so."

*   *   *

I just couldn't bring myself to ask Drew. I guess it was my self-confidence—or lack of it—at work once again. I hinted that maybe he'd like to do something Saturday night, though. My treat.

"I can't Saturday night, Jordan. I'd love to, but I can't. Why don't we go out Friday instead? But I want to treat. And wear something fancy."

Friday sounded like a wonderful consolation prize. I tried to tell myself that just being with Drew was the most important thing, but the part of me that had never experienced a high school dance was a little bit disappointed.

"We're not going," I told Carrie and Pam.

"What do you mean you're not going?" Carrie asked. "You have to go. We planned it."

"Drew is busy Saturday night," I said. "We're going out Friday night instead."

"Busy doing what?" Pam asked.

"Pam, I didn't ask. I didn't think it was any of my business. If Drew had wanted me to know, he would have told me."

"You won't see me in my dress," Pam whined. "And I look so good in it."

"Of course I'll see you. I'll come over before you leave, or you can stop by on your way to the dance. Or if that doesn't work out, I'll see your dance pictures later." That seemed to satisfy Pam, but Carrie still looked a little upset.

"I wanted you to see my date," Carrie said.

"I'll see his picture too," I told her.

"I know," she said glumly. "But I wanted you to see him in *person*."

*   *   *

"Is my best girl ready?" Drew asked. "Wow! You look terrific," he said. I was wearing a new skirt and sweater outfit in a pale shade of coral. I felt almost pretty in it. Drew had gotten dressed up too. I could smell his after-shave lotion and his blond hair was still damp from his shower.

"Thank you," I said. "And what do you mean by your *best* girl?" I teased.

He held open the car door for me, and we just stood there for a minute. "Jordan," he finally said, "I want you to know you are my *only* girl. No matter what."

"No matter what," I said and got in the car. He slammed the door and leaned in through my window.

"Do you believe me?" he asked.

"Of course I believe you, Drew. Why wouldn't I believe you?" Why was he asking me such funny questions? I wondered.

He got in on his side of the car and started the engine.

"Where are we going?" I asked.

He leaned over and kissed me softly, a kiss that lingered. "I'm taking you out to dinner," he said finally.

We went to the Seafood Cellar. The atmosphere seemed a lot more romantic, more exciting with Drew than it had been with my parents. "This is my favorite restaurant," I told him.

"I know," he said. His blue eyes glistened in the candlelight.

"I wasn't expecting a fancy dinner," I said.

"I wanted to make this a special night," he said.

"Every night is special with you, Drew."

He took my hand. "I feel that way about you too, Jordan. And, well, I just wanted you to know."

I looked around the room. The saltwater aquariums held some exotically colored clown and butterfly fish. "I love it here," I told Drew. "And someday I'm going to have a saltwater aquarium of my own. Freshwater fish just aren't as colorful."

"What do you want to eat?" Drew asked me. "It seems a shame to order fish after staring at them in their homes."

"That's right," I said. "Make me feel guilty about my dinner."

Drew laughed. "They just seem so vulnerable somehow."

"Well, I'm not ordering clown fish or seahorse." Actually, I wasn't hungry at all.

The waiter brought our salads and dropped mine on the floor. Drew deadpanned, "What is it about you? Every time I take you out, someone spills something all over the floor."

"It's my stunning beauty," I retorted. "It shakes them all up."

When our dinners arrived, my head and my heart were deadlocked in battle: my head sent messages to my stomach, telling it to eat every bite; but my heart sent messages too, saying it was okay for my stomach to be jumpy and too nervous to eat. In the end, they compromised. I relaxed enough to finally eat some of my dinner.

After dessert we walked out onto the restaurant's garden terrace and looked down at the city below. We were alone on the balcony—they didn't open it for dining until the first of June.

"The city looks like a giant's jewel box from up here," I said. "Aren't the lights beautiful?" I shivered in the cold and Drew took his coat off and put it over my shoulders.

"Better?" he asked.

I nodded.

"Jordan?" he said. He pulled me close to him. We stood like that a moment, neither one of us saying anything. I could feel his heart thump against my cheek. "Jordan, there's something I want to tell you."

I looked up at him. He seemed to be struggling with something. "What, Drew? What is it?"

He wrapped his arms tighter around me. "It's . . . it's nothing," he said finally. "Except . . . except that I love you." His warm mouth searched for mine and he kissed me, more intently than ever before.

"That's not nothing, Drew," I was finally able to answer. "That's a pretty big something."

"I know," he said. "I just want you to remember it, Jordan. No matter what."

"How could I forget?"

We turned and walked slowly back to the parking lot. I felt good with Drew's strong arm around me. Yet I could tell something was bothering him. But what?

Chapter Eleven

Sunday, bright and early, the telephone rang. "Jordan?" Carrie said. "It's me. I spent the night at Pam's. We want to know if you're going to church."

"I think so. How was the dance?"

"It was great. Ten or eleven o'clock service?"

"Ten probably."

"Okay. We didn't want to miss you. We want to see you and tell you all about . . . everything."

"Okay. I'll meet you in front of the parish hall. So tell me, what was Don's cousin Willy like?"

"He was nice."

"That's all? Just nice?"

"He was okay. Sort of big, though."

"He's huge," Pam broke in. "He plays tackle for Madison High. I think he scared Carrie."

"He did not."

"Yeah, well how come you spent half the night in the bathroom?"

The two of them began to argue over the extension.

"Listen, I'll see you two later, okay? You can fill me in on everything." I hung up the phone and searched my closet for something clean to wear to church.

*   *   *

Pam and Carrie were waiting for me when I got to church. Mom and Dad went directly into the sanctuary, and Jessica and Jimmy ran to their Sunday school classroom.

"You going to Sunday school or to the service?" Pam asked me.

"Where are you two going?" I asked.

"Wherever you are," Carrie said.

"Well, if you want to talk, we can't very well go to the service. Mom will kill me if I giggle in church one more time."

"I don't think you'll be giggling," Carrie said.

I studied her carefully, but her face was expressionless.

"Let's go to Sunday school then," Pam said quickly. "That group never gets started on time anyway."

We walked around the parish hall and sat on the bench outside our classroom, waiting for everyone to arrive. Pam sat on one side of me and Carrie on the other.

"All right, you two," I said. "You've got me surrounded. I give up."

Neither one of them spoke.

"What in the world is the matter?"

Silence.

"Will one of you please tell me what's going on? What happened at the dance last night to make you two so shy?"

"You tell her, Pam."

"No. You tell her."

"Well, *one* of you better tell me and soon. I can't stand the suspense."

Pam started slowly. "It's just that we don't know *how* to tell you."

Carrie added, "We weren't going to tell you at all, only we figured it would be better for you to hear it from us rather than someone else."

"Hear *what?*"

"It's about Drew."

My heart thudded in my chest. I was surprised they couldn't hear it. "What about him?" I asked.

"He was at the dance last night, Jordan." Pam looked as though she might burst into tears at any moment.

"By himself?" I had to know.

"No. He was with a girl that neither of us had ever seen before." Carrie looked miserable, about the way I was feeling.

"That big creep," Pam said. "I don't know how he could do this to you."

"They hardly danced at all," Carrie said. I knew she was trying to make me feel better.

"Just a couple of slow dances and then they just sat and talked."

"They didn't dance real close or anything, Jordan. I watched them." Carrie looked at me sympathetically.

"Yeah, I noticed that too," Pam said. "It was more like he was dancing with his sister. Does he have a sister?"

"No."

"Oh."

"What did she look like?" I asked.

Mr. Bond stuck his head out of the door. "Are you ladies going to join us this morning?" He smiled, a big grin that revealed his big white teeth. "Or," he continued, "shall we come outside and join you?"

The three of us stood up. Mr. Bond returned his attention to the classroom.

"What did she look like?" I repeated. We sat down at the back of the room.

"She had short dark hair and big brown eyes," Pam said. "She was cute, but she was sort of skinny. She reminded me of a little girl dressed up in her mother's clothes."

"She sure had big eyes," Carrie whispered.

"Susie," I said gloomily.

"Please open this week's Bible study booklet to page three," Mr. Bond said.

At first I didn't know what to think. I sat through Sunday school in a complete daze. I was thankful Mr. Bond didn't call on me. I guess he realized it was no use trying to penetrate the fog.

My first reaction was sorrow. I was hurt that Drew would pull something so crummy. It didn't seem like him. And it didn't fit in with Friday night.

Friday night. Maybe the dance was what he'd been trying to tell me about that night. Tears welled in my eyes. I could feel their hot warmth threatening to drip down my face. *Why?* I wiped at my eyes with the back of my hand. I didn't want Carrie or Pam or any of the other kids to see me crying.

Why? I asked myself again. We weren't going steady, true, but he had said he loved me. I blew my nose. Carrie and Pam both looked in my direction. And he had given me the necklace. That had to count for something.

I fingered the thin filagree chain that held the tiny gold heart. I reached up behind my neck and loosened the clasp. The necklace fell free in my hand.

I stared at the perfect pearl and realized what a perfect jerk I'd been. Suddenly, my hurt was replaced by rage. Pure and simple. It was a more satisfying emotion, easier to deal with.

The necklace nestled safely in the pocket section of my purse, and I concentrated on just what I was going to say to Drew. *If* I ever talked to him again.

*   *   *

Monday morning I made a special effort to get to school early. I walked down the stairs to the basement floor of the old building, my heart pounding wildly. I looked around. The hall was practically deserted.

I was really nervous, and it took me three tries to get Drew's combination. Finally I heard the magic click and felt the latch give beneath my fingers.

I opened the door. My books were hopelessly scrambled with his. I took out all my things, taking a second look to make sure I had everything.

The hall was starting to fill with students. Quickly I reached into my purse and extracted the necklace. I hung it on the coat hook and watched for a second while it swung back and forth. The weight of the heart pressed downward and the necklace stopped moving. My own heart pressed against my chest and I felt an unfamiliar, dull ache growing inside. I slammed the locker door and ran quickly to the girls' bathroom where the cold tiled walls provided only temporary sanctuary. Sooner or later I would have to see Drew. I hoped it would be later.

I did manage to avoid him for the first half of the day, but he caught up with me at lunch. I was standing in line by myself when I felt a strong grip on my arm. I turned around to face an intense, angry Drew. "Let go of me," I said. "You're hurting my arm."

He held on, only loosened his grip. With his other hand he fished in his pocket and withdrew the necklace. He dangled it in front of me. "What's this supposed to mean?" he asked.

"Exactly what you think it means." I jerked away from him quickly and pushed through the crowd.

"Jordan!" He caught up with me instantly. "We need to talk."

"I don't think so," I said.

"It's your stupid jealousy again, isn't it?"

"It's my justifiable anger," I retorted and kept walking.

"There's no need to be angry if you'd only hear me out."

"I'm not interested in hearing you out. As far as I'm concerned, we have absolutely nothing to say to each other."

He grabbed my arm again. I yanked it quickly away. "Jordan! Wait!"

I didn't wait. There was nothing to wait for. Once again I marched into the girls' bathroom and stayed there until well after the bell rang.

Chapter Twelve

I'm back to hugging Julius. He doesn't hug back, like Drew, but at least he never hurts my feelings.

I've tried to keep busy. I cleaned out my closet, throwing away about five years' worth of old clothes that had somehow accumulated in there. Some I gave to Jessica, some to the Goodwill, and some were so bad they went straight into Mom's scrap bag.

I found things I hadn't even thought about in years, like my Halloween costume from fifth grade, the year I dressed up like the Cat in the Hat. What was I saving it for? I think I've inherited more than my share of Mom's sentimentality. She saves everything. For her, everything has some sort of connection to the past. She still has all my *kindergarten* papers!

My dad is just the opposite. He doesn't like clutter or mess. All of his tools hang neatly in the garage, and all his nails and bolts are separated and individually categorized. He keeps them in labeled coffee cans. When Mom borrows a hammer or the pliers and forgets to put them back,

Dad really freaks out. For Mother's Day I think I'm going to buy Mom her very own hammer.

It's tough knowing I'm now committed to ROP, especially since Drew was the deciding factor. Actually, I only have a few more weeks to go until I get my certificate. I'm still not sure I'm nurse or doctor material, though.

I had just finished sorting through my things when Mom came walking down the hall. "May I come in?" she asked.

I nodded.

"Jordan, I'm so happy to see you taking an interest in keeping your room clean. But why the sudden change?"

"I guess I just got tired of living with the dust balls, Mom."

"Oh, look, there's your Cat in the Hat costume. I remember when I made that for you. You looked so cute in it. What are you going to do with it?"

"I don't know," I said. "Maybe give it to Jessica." I had been planning to throw it out but suddenly realized I couldn't do that.

"I hope it will fit her. Oh, I almost forgot. Carrie called for you. And there's a plate of brownies on the counter."

I could see the memories floating behind Mom's eyes as she fingered my old costume. Even in my deep depression, brownies sounded good. I headed for the kitchen to call Carrie and to ease my pain with a big dose of chocolate.

*   *   *

"Hi," Carrie said. "I'm glad you called back. I found some interesting information. Hang on a sec, okay, while I go get it."

"Okay." I helped myself to a brownie.

"Back again. I have it right here. Somewhere." I could hear her searching through some pages. "What are you eating?" she asked.

"Brownies."

"Lucky. The only snacks we have are carrot and celery sticks. My mom's on this big 'we're all going to lose weight' kick."

I pictured Carrie gnawing away on a carrot and at the same time drooling over my brownie.

"Here it is. Right here. It says that once a gift is given to a woman by a man she has no responsibility to return it just because the relationship has dissolved. You could have kept the necklace, Jordan."

"I didn't want to keep it. It didn't seem right."

"Yeah, but now Drew could turn around and give it to some other girl. For all you know, you weren't the first owner."

"Thanks a lot."

"Well?"

"Drew wouldn't do something like that. He's not that big a crumb. Anyway, are you suggesting I ask for it back?"

"I guess that would be sort of awkward," she admitted.

"I guess so," I answered sarcastically.

"Well, just keep this information under your hat for future reference." She said it brightly in her "all is not lost" voice.

"Thank you, Carrie. I will. I'm sure it will come in handy if in the future I decide to get engaged and unengaged."

"My thoughts exactly. A girl could collect a lot of jewelry that way."

* * *

Just as I successfully avoided Drew, which was made simple by the fact that he wasn't in class the next Saturday, I also practiced avoiding Otto. I had learned quickly to identify his lumbering footsteps in the halls, and I got pretty good at ducking into patients' rooms whenever I saw—or heard—him approaching.

The other girls thought I was nuts; I guess they weren't James Bond fans. But Otto really scared me. There was no way around it.

Mr. Harris was due to be discharged to a convalescent home. The hospital had done all that was medically possible for him, and in fact, he seemed to be improving. I decided to take him for a last tour of the grounds. As we approached the service elevator I said, "You'll be discharged soon, Mr. Harris. Won't that be nice?"

Mr. Harris didn't answer.

"Won't that be nice?" I said a little louder.

Still no response. I walked around in front of him. His head slumped forward. He was asleep.

I was so busy with Mr. Harris that I failed to notice the service elevator doors open. When I looked up, it was straight into Otto's eyes. "Hi missy," he said, grinning at me. Otto was standing next to a gurney. "I'm taking Mrs. Shelkopf back to her room," he told me. "She's just had her X-rays, haven't you, Mrs. Shelkopf?"

I figured it was safe on the elevator with Otto as long as we both had patients with us, so I reluctantly wheeled Mr. Harris in. I stared hard at Mrs. Shelkopf, a pale, gray-haired woman. She didn't look too good. The doors shut.

"Is she sleeping?" I asked Otto hopefully.

"Nope," he replied.

"Is she dead?" I asked weakly.

"Just unconscious," he said.

"How come you talk to her if she's unconscious?" I asked, very much wanting to believe him.

"I talk to all the patients," he said. "Who's to say she can't hear me? Right, Mrs. Shelkopf?" He patted her hand.

The elevator lurched upward. I clung desperately to the back of the wheelchair. Wild thoughts ran through my head. Maybe Mrs. Shelkopf was dead. Maybe Otto had killed her. Just as he planned to kill me. Maybe she'd been fine just an hour ago. Maybe . . .

The elevator ground to a halt. Mr. Harris's head bobbed on his chest. "What's the matter?" I asked Otto. I positioned myself on the far side of the elevator. If Otto wanted to come after me, he'd have to climb over Mrs. Shelkopf and Mr. Harris first.

"I don't know," Otto said. He banged on the service panel.

Nothing.

"Bang again," I directed from the questionable safety of my corner. Otto pushed harder on the buttons.

"I am," he answered. I thought I detected a note of panic in his voice. Or was it excitement? "It's getting hot in here." His voice quivered.

Oh no! Quick, Jordan! Think! Here you are, stuck between floors in the hospital elevator with sleeping Mr. Harris, unconscious (dead?) Mrs. Shelkopf, and sex-maniac (killer?) Otto. What to do?

Don't panic. Faint. That's it, faint. Maybe he'll leave you alone when he sees you all white and pasty and sweating on the floor.

"I'm feeling faint," I said weakly.

"You can't faint!" he wailed. Sweat poured from Otto's brow. He unbuttoned his shirt.

"Why can't I?" I demanded. I squeezed closer to the corner.

"I'm going to need you in a minute," Otto whispered.

His eyes bulged. He was breathing rapidly. If I didn't know better, I'd say he was hyperventilating.

"What for?" I asked.

"To get me *out* of here. I'm claustrophobic!" he screamed. "I can't breathe!" He leaned against the wall of the elevator, gasping for air.

"You're kidding," I said. "You mean you're not going to kill me?"

"Help me," he gasped. His feet gave way under him, and he collapsed to the floor.

"You mean you didn't kill Mrs. Shelkopf?"

He tugged frantically at his collar. "Help me, please!"

It was a difficult decision to make, but ultimately instinct (or nurse's training, I'm not sure which) took over. Otto really did look as though he could use some assistance. I squeezed past Mr. Harris and Mrs. Shelkopf. (Was she still breathing?)

And then, right in front of me, Otto passed out cold. *Now what?* I had studied hard for nurse's training—in fact, I was getting an A—but we hadn't yet gotten to the chapter "Big Lummox Passes Out in Elevator."

Quick, Jordan. *Think.* A tourniquet? No, he's not bleeding. C.P.R.? Has he had a heart attack? I moved closer to Otto and peered cautiously at his now still form. Maybe he was faking it.

"It was Din, Din, Din," Mr. Harris suddenly shouted, scaring me half to death.

"It's okay, Mr. Harris," I reassured him, although I had no idea what I meant by that.

Otto looked comfortable enough. I hated to touch him, but . . . but . . . I leaned down close to him. Smelling salts, that's what I needed. I didn't have any. I did have a wrinkled hanky in my apron pocket that smelled like my Innocence Lost perfume, but I didn't dare wave *that* under his nose. And then, the answer. Mouth-to-mouth, that was it. But could I? With Otto?

I pulled back his upper lip. His teeth looked normal enough. Funny. What had happened to all those metal caps?

Now *I* was the one hyperventilating. Calm down, Jordan, I told myself. You can do this. You have to do this. A life may depend on it. I pinched Otto's nostrils shut, leaned over him, and closed my eyes.

"It was Din, Din, Din," Mr. Harris shouted again.

Suddenly the elevator lurched and then jerked upward. I sat back on my knees. The movement stopped and the door slid open. Fresh air rushed in. I gasped it thankfully. And then I looked up. A nurse, a maintenance man, an orderly, and Miss Piaget were all staring at me.

Miss Piaget was the first to speak. "Jordan," she said sternly, coming toward me. "What on earth have you done to poor Otto?"

I knew I should have taken electronics.

Chapter Thirteen

Miss Piaget waved some smelling salts under *my* nose, I guess to calm me down. I jerked my head away from the stinging smell, but I still couldn't stop blubbering.

"Jordan, please try to control yourself," she said. "Mrs. Shelkopf isn't dead. Whatever gave you that idea? And Otto is fine. He just fainted." Miss Piaget sat with her arm around me.

"Fainted?" I asked. How sneaky could he get, using *my* trick! Did he think I was going to harm *him?*

"Yes. I guess he's claustrophobic. The four of you were in there quite a while, you know. Luckily, I was still in the hospital when I found out that the elevator was stuck and that a patient and student of mine were missing. You did fine, Jordan. Under the circumstances, you really kept your head."

"I did?"

"Yes. Otto told us how you helped him."

"He did?"

"Yes, he did."

"What did he say I helped him *with?*" I asked, curious now. I sniffled, and she handed me a tissue.

"He said you displayed extraordinary calm when he became frantic."

"Otto said all that?"

"Jordan, why do you keep questioning what Otto said? Did anything else happen in that elevator?"

I shook my head. All the really awful things I remembered hadn't really happened. I guess I must have come pretty close to fainting myself. Otto hadn't really chased me up and down the halls, threatening to tie me to the gurney with stethoscopes. He hadn't built a wall of bed pans and buried me behind them. He hadn't stuffed me down the laundry chute where even James Bond couldn't find me. Poor Otto, I really had read him wrong. He's as harmless as Julius.

"Miss Piaget, could I go home now? I'm not feeling too terrific after all this excitement."

"Of course, Jordan. I'd be happy to drive you."

"What about Mr. Harris?"

"He was taken back up to geriatrics. I understand he's due to be released soon."

I nodded.

"It's always nice to see your patients recuperate enough to leave the hospital, isn't it?"

I nodded again. We stood up. Miss Piaget still had her arm around me, I guess for support. Did she think I was a total basket case?

"I'm all right now, Miss Piaget, honest."

*   *   *

I sat huddled in the front seat of Miss Piaget's sports car. Somehow it wasn't the automobile I'd visualized her in. An old station wagon seemed more appropriate. I wondered if perhaps she had a whole other life away from the hospital. It certainly was possible, and my experience today had taught me how deceiving appearances could be. I was so sure that Otto was a tiger, and it turns out he's just an old pussycat with claustrophobia.

Miss Piaget chatted away non-stop. Outside the class-room, she seemed positively cheery. I couldn't wait to tell the other kids. She still wore her whistle, but I was getting used to seeing it around her neck.

She deposited me on my doorstep matter-of-factly. I could just as easily have been a bottle of milk or the evening newspaper. She handled everything with the same efficiency.

Of course my family was curious about my experience.

"Was it scary?" Jimmy asked.

"Was it hot in there?" Jessica wanted to know. "I can't stand hot elevators, because sometimes a really smelly person gets on next to you and then you can't breathe."

"Jessica!" Mom said.

Dad chuckled.

"Oh, I just meant like an old-lady perfumy smell, Mom. You know, like at the department store. There's always one or two women walking around who stink like dead roses."

I knew what Jessica meant. A perfume fog, I called it.

I passed the rolls to Dad. "Did you jump up at the last minute?" he teased.

"Oh, Daddy!"

"Well, we're glad you're safe and sound," Mom said. "That must have been a hair-raising experience."

"Especially for Otto," I joked. "It was so hair raising, he doesn't have his anymore."

Daddy really laughed at that.

*   *   *

I guess Otto or Miss Piaget had spread the word because by the next Saturday everyone at the hospital was treating me like some kind of a celebrity. As I walked down the corridors I kept hearing the whispers: "There goes the girl who helped Otto," or "That's the kid who was stuck in the elevator."

The notoriety didn't change my work status though. I still had to work hard if I wanted to get my certificate. And making beds and wheeling gurneys around isn't easy.

I guess it was fate or something that I just happened to be the aide who was sent on an errand to the first floor. The head nurse motioned me over to her desk. I saw her quickly glance at my name tag. "Jordan, would you please go down to Admissions for me? Mrs. O'Hara's rings should have been placed in the safe. Somehow it wasn't taken care of when she was admitted." She handed me a small package.

After my elevator experience, I decided to use the stairs whenever I could. If I had to move a patient, I would wait and sneak them onto the main floor elevator. And stairs were good exercise, especially five floors' worth.

I handed the package to the admitting clerk and gave her the patient's name and room number. Then, as I turned to make my way back to the stairs, I saw Susie. She was paler than I remembered.

A sick feeling weighed heavy in my stomach. She indicated with a wave of her hand that she wanted me to come over. Well, it was Drew I was mad at, not Susie.

I walked over, a stern resolve my invisible crutch.

"Hi," I said cheerfully. I hoped no note of falseness had sounded in my voice. "What are you doing here? I thought you were discharged weeks ago."

"Oh, the same old routine," she said. "I'm back for more tests. And every time we have to go through the same process." She gestured toward Admitting. A man and a woman sat close together, talking to one of the clerks.

"Your parents?" I asked.

She nodded. "I'm glad I got to see you again, Jordan. I wanted to tell you what a nice boyfriend I think you have. You two make such a cute couple." She smiled at me. A thought ran through my head that the "other woman" is supposed to be a real witch. Susie was making this hard. She certainly didn't fit the stock character description. Was it possible she knew nothing of the wall between Drew and me? I searched her face for clues, but could see no sign of insincerity there.

"It was so sweet of Drew to take me to the dance. I had a lot of fun. I'd never been to a dance before, and it was wonderful."

I felt like a crumb. "I'm glad you enjoyed it, Susie."

"Drew told me that you and he had discussed it and you wanted me to go too." Her big eyes looked into mine. "And, well . . . I just wanted to thank you for lending your boyfriend to me for the evening. At first I was sort of worried about it, but Drew said your relationship was so special that nothing could come between—"

I interrupted her. "*Drew* said that?"

She looked at me questioningly. "Yes, but—"

My heart pounding with excitement, I leaned over and hugged her. "Gosh, Susie, thank you. I've got to go now, okay? I guess I'll see you around."

"Say hello to Drew for me," she said.

I waved good-bye and ran to the stairs. "I will," I called back. "I will."

I took the stairs two at a time, happiness forcing me onward. At the third-floor landing, I stopped, out of breath. What if it was too late? What if Drew never wanted to speak to me again?

I *had* acted like a jerk. He *did* care for me. There really was some explanation for Susie, and I hadn't let him tell me. But what? I couldn't wait to hear.

*   *   *

I phoned Drew as soon as I got home. He was out. "May I take a message?" a warm, feminine voice said. In spite of the soothing sound of his mother's voice, I panicked and barely managed to squeak out that I would call back.

But I knew I wouldn't call again. It had taken all my nerve to dial those seven numbers the first time. I had no nerve left. I paced. I brooded. I criticized myself. Finally I went into my room and lay down on my bed.

I hugged Julius. One of his paws was coming off. The years of constant, continuous companionship had taken their toll. I poked the fuzzy stuffing back into place and searched my desk drawer for a needle and thread. I didn't have brown, so I used black. "Now, Julius," I said, "this will only sting for an instant. And then you'll be as good as new." I carefully tacked his paw back on. The black stitches only showed if you looked closely. I tied the final knot and cut the thread. "There now, Julius. All better."

Julius didn't respond, although I swear he looked happier. I kissed my silent friend and wished I could mend my broken relationship with Drew as easily.

Why couldn't I have believed in myself just a little bit more? Drew had apparently believed in me enough to think I could handle his date with Susie. But then why hadn't he told me in advance? Perhaps he had tried. And I still didn't know why he'd asked Susie to the dance in the first place.

There were too many unresolved questions, and only Drew knew the answers. I fell asleep dreaming about him.

*   *   *

"So what do I do now, Carrie?" I had just told her everything—the encounter with Susie, the conversation, the whole bit.

"How should I know, Jordan? Do you think I'm your romantic advisor or something?"

"You've always helped me in the past."

"Well, the past was always in the abstract; I knew you'd never act on it. This is reality. Whatever happens, you'll blame me."

"Or thank you?" I said hopefully.

"Fat chance."

"You think I flubbed up *that* bad?"

"Let's just say I don't want to be involved."

"But why not? You've always been involved before. In fact, you were always butting your nose in, whether I wanted you to or not."

"Is that any way to talk to a friend?"

"Help me. That's all I ask."

Carrie shook her blond curls. "Oh, for goodness' sake," she said.

"Then you'll help?"

Carrie stopped walking and turned to face me. "I'll think of something. I might need to read up on it, though, and that might take a while.''

"Oh, thank you, Carrie.'' I hugged her.

"Hey, cut it out, will you? You're wrinkling my new blouse.''

* * *

It took her until lunchtime to solve my problem. I was sitting alone on a bench, not really hungry, but feeling guilty about wasting food. I stuffed my uneaten apple back into the brown bag and searched the crowds for Drew.

A quick tap on my shoulder startled me, and I turned around abruptly. Carrie was standing there. She had a firm grip on Drew's arm.

"I figured if I had to read about it, we'd never solve anything, so I opted for the direct approach.'' She shoved him toward me. "Drew, Jordan. Jordan, Drew. Now that you've met, I think you two have something to talk about. Well, see ya.'' And off she went.

"Carrie!'' I called after her, but it was a futile effort. She quickly disappeared into the crowd.

Drew sat down next to me. "Hello, Jordan,'' he said softly. I stared into his eyes. I had almost forgotten what a deep blue they were.

Drew smiled at me then, and suddenly I knew everything was going to be all right. Somehow we would work things out. "I'm glad you're finally willing to talk to me. What was Carrie rattling on about? She had to read up on what?''

"On a hundred different ways to say I'm sorry,'' I said.

"Come on,'' he said, standing up and gently tugging on my hand. "Let's go outside and sit on the grass. I guess I have some explaining to do.''

I grabbed my lunch bag and books. "Want an apple?" I asked him. "An apple a day keeps the doctor away, you know."

"No thanks," he said, still holding tightly to my hand. "This doctor-to-be doesn't want to go away. At least not from you."

Chapter Fourteen

We walked to the grassy hill in front of the school and sat down. "Jordan," Drew said, "I'm sorry if I hurt you. I never meant to."

"I know that, Drew. I just don't understand why you took Susie to the dance."

"I had every intention of asking you. But while I was working in the hospital the Saturday before the dance, I overheard a conversation about Susie that really jolted me. Her parents and a doctor were talking in the hall. The doctor said the tests were nonconclusive, and Susie's mom asked if that meant Susie would get better. The doctor said that at this point, they just didn't know. It really shook me up, Jordan."

"I can understand that. But why didn't you tell me?"

"There were a lot of reasons, I guess. Number one, up until that time the hospital work for me had been mainly fun. I guess I just never confronted the possibility that some patients don't get better. I decided I wanted to do something for Susie. Something special because she's been so brave and so positive throughout the whole ordeal. I asked her to the dance knowing she would be out of the hospital by then.

"I wanted to talk it over with you. Honest. I even tried—the night we went out to dinner, and before that. But I was afraid you wouldn't understand. I saw how jealous you were . . ."

There it was again, my lack of self-confidence ruining everything.

"And you had no reason to be jealous, not really. So then I rationalized that maybe you'd never know. I guess I tried to take the easy way out. I didn't count on your friends showing up at the dance. It was a stupid thing to do because it came between us."

"No it wasn't," I said finally. "It was a nice thing for you to do for Susie. But you're right. I probably wouldn't have handled it very well. Proof of that is, I *didn't* handle it well. I didn't even give you a chance to explain."

Just then the bell rang. "Jordan," Drew said, getting to his feet and pulling me up after him. "I want you to take this back." He reached into his pocket and withdrew the necklace. "No matter what happens in the future, I want you to have it. I gave it to you as a birthday gift. It's yours. Will you take it back?"

I was afraid to speak, afraid my voice would come out all squeaky and strange. But I managed to nod my head.

"Turn around then," he said, "and I'll put it on you." Once again the fragile heart hung safely around my neck. "We're going to be late for class," Drew said. "But I don't really care."

At that point, neither did I.

*   *   *

"I see you've resolved your differences," Pam said. She stared at my necklace and then cuddled closer to Don Pomerantz. "Oh, I won't be walking home today. Don is taking me," she said, giving him a loving look.

"Want a ride?" he asked, more out of politeness than a real desire to take me home.

"No thanks," I said. "I need the exercise."

After school Drew took the bus to work and Carrie and I began the trudge home.

"Do you think we'll remember these walks when we're old ladies?" Carrie asked.

"I don't know. What do you think?"

"Sometimes I already feel like an old lady," she said. "An old *spinster* lady."

"Oh, come off it."

"I'm not kidding, Jordan. You've got Drew, and now even Pam has someone."

"Your time will come."

"You sound like my mother."

"What about Don's cousin? What was his name?"

"Willy," she said glumly. "He scared me half to death."

I had to chuckle. "So Pam was right about that."

"Yeah, but don't tell her. He was just so . . . so big," she said. She thought a moment, then amended, "Not just big. Gargantuan."

"You can't be afraid of someone just because of his size," I said. I told her about Otto.

"Gosh, Jordan, you actually thought he was going to hurt you?"

"Yes. And the more I think about it, the more I realize that *I'm* the one who probably hurt him. Everyone at the hospital says he's very sensitive. Do you think I ought to apologize?"

"For what?" she asked. "For believing he was a mass murderer? How are you going to do that? You can't very well walk up to him and say, 'Otto, I'm sorry I thought you were Jack the Ripper.' That's worse than saying nothing."

"I guess you're right."

"You'll think of some way out of this. You always do."

"No," I said. "You'll think of something for me. You're a better thinker."

We were at the street corner where we go our separate ways. I hugged her.

"Oh for goodness' sake," she said. "What did you do that for?"

"Just for being my friend," I said. "For being you."

*   *   *

True to form, Carrie did think of something. She decided I ought to have a party for all the nursing attendants, a certification party.

"That way you could invite Otto and sort of make it up to him," she said. "You could also invite some of the other orderlies. Any cute ones?" she asked.

"A party might be a good idea," I said. "It would be fun. Maybe I could even invite some of the discharged patients. I'll have to ask Mom."

"Wait a minute," Carrie said. "This was my idea. If it's just a hospital party, how am I going to be able to come?"

"You can be the caterer," I joked.

"Very funny."

"Don't worry about it," I said. "I'll introduce you to Miss Piaget as next semester's enrollee."

"Jordan, you know I'm not nurse material."

"You think I am? I just set my sights higher. Dr. Collins, I presume?"

"No offense, Jordan, but I'd prefer to just lay down and die rather than have you touch this perfect body. The thought of you with a scalpel makes me shudder. You can't even cut a straight line with scissors."

"It just takes practice, my dear." I made snipping motions in her direction.

"I pity your first patients," she said.

"I already practiced on Julius, and he didn't complain."

"Julius is definitely not the complaining type," she said.

Chapter Fifteen

"For the past few years, class, every ROP group that has gone through this hospital has had a fund-raiser of some sort to commemorate its time spent at West Valley." Miss Piaget looked out over the class. "Last semester's group had a book fair and used the funds to purchase a new supply of puzzles and games for the pediatrics ward. A few years before that a class held a bike-a-thon and purchased a plaque for the East Wing. Take a look at it the next time you're through there. Now I want you to think about something you'd like to do for the hospital."

Chris raised her hand. "I think we should buy something useful. A plaque is silly. No one can do anything with it. I think that would be a waste of money."

"I agree," Wendy said. "Let's get something the hospital patients would really enjoy."

"How about a big shade tree for the garden area?" one girl suggested.

"But the Garden Club provides that sort of thing free of charge," Chris argued.

"What if we bought a TV for the pediatrics playroom?" Drew said.

"I'm not sure that's such a good idea, Drew," I said tentatively. "The kids already have televisions in their rooms and probably watch too much already. I think the playroom should be a place where they can get away from that influence."

"Do you have any suggestions, Jordan?" Miss Piaget asked me.

I thought for a moment. "Well," I said finally, "I've noticed that the patients on the geriatrics ward all respond to music. They love it when I sing to them. What if we bought a stereo for the sun room?"

"I think that's a terrific idea," Chris said excitedly.

"Me too," Drew added.

"Any other ideas?" Miss Piaget scanned the room. No hands went up. "Then is it settled? A stereo for the sun room?"

"Maybe we could even get Randall's Music Shop to donate a few records," Wendy said.

"Now the big question," Miss Piaget said, "is how to raise the money."

"What about a bake sale?" a dark-haired girl in the back suggested.

"Oh, bake sales are so boring," Chris whined. "Everyone has them. Besides, we'd have to sell an awful lot of cookies and brownies to buy a stereo."

"Chris is right," Drew said. "What about a fair with games and an auction and a white-elephant sale? Every year my church puts on a fair, and they make hundreds of dollars."

"But I bet they start planning for it months in advance, right, Drew?" Miss Piaget asked.

Drew looked glum. "Yeah, I guess you're right. I

forgot about that. My father is on the organizing committee, and they meet for weeks and weeks beforehand.''

"Let's not take any more time with this now," Miss Piaget said. "We have a lot to cover today. But I want you to think about it during the week and have some concrete suggestions for the next time we meet. As soon as we come up with an idea, we'll need to organize into groups and get this thing going. If there are no volunteers, I'd like to appoint Jordan as chairperson. Any objections?''

I looked around the room. No volunteers came forth. They weren't dumb. With finals coming up soon, no one in his or her right mind wanted an additional burden. Thanks a lot, Miss Piaget.

"And now," she said briskly, "let's get back to work, shall we? Jordan, see me after class and I'll give you my phone number in case someone comes up with an idea before next week. We need to get started on this." She turned her back to the class and picked up a piece of chalk. "Who remembers the procedure used when dealing with a small child who is choking?"

Notebooks clattered open, and a few pencils dropped. It was back to business. And I was left with the business of coming up with a unique, profitable fund-raiser.

*   *   *

The sun was warm on our backs as Drew and I started the long walk home. "Looks like Miss Piaget handed you a real tough one," Drew said.

"That's just how I feel," I said. "That she handed it to *me* exclusively."

"We'll think of something," he said positively. "Don't worry about it." I liked the fact that Drew said "we." It made the job seem less awesome.

"To earn enough to buy a stereo we're going to have to generate a lot of interest," I mused. "That means something fun. Which leaves out walk-a-thons, et cetera. They've been done a thousand times before. We need something new."

"I think it should be somehow related to the hospital, don't you?" he asked.

"Like what, Drew?"

"Oh, I don't know. A raffle where you win a solid gold stethoscope or a contest where you guess how many tonsils will be removed in a single week. That sort of thing."

I couldn't help giggling. "Right," I said. "Both of those would be big sellers, I'm sure of it. Ladies and gentlemen, step right up and place your bets on how many stitches it takes to sew up the fat lady's appendectomy."

"Internal or external?" Drew joked.

I socked him playfully.

"Maybe we could bottle your iced tea and sell it as a magic elixir guaranteed to cure all ills. Good for man or beast."

I socked him again. "I don't appreciate your reference to my iced tea," I said. "There's nothing wrong with it."

"Oh, no?" he asked. "It looks like water from the bottom of the ocean."

"Very funny," I told him, feigning indignation. (I really can't make decent iced tea.)

"Well, we'll think of something."

We turned the corner onto my block and were almost run over by Jessica and Jimmy barreling down the sidewalk on their roller skates. Drew and I both jumped simultaneously off the curb.

"I've got it!" I squealed, thrilled with my sudden streak of genius.

Jimmy and Jessica buzzed around the corner.

"And those two gave it to me."

*   *   *

"We're having a wheelchair race," I explained to the gathered class. "I've already okayed it with Miss Piaget. The hospital is willing to donate the wheelchairs on the condition that Drew's dad draws up some sort of insurance policy against damage. We've talked to Parks and Recreation, and they're agreeable to letting us hold the race in the Sycamore Creek parking lot. Miss Piaget thought it might be fun if the teams that raced against each other were hospital staff. You know, the orderlies versus the nurses versus the doctors versus ROP."

A cheer went up. "Great idea!" Wendy yelled.

"We need to have some tickets printed," I went on.

"I'll take care of that," Chris volunteered. "My uncle is a printer. Probably we'll only have to pay for the paper."

"Great. We also need a sales force to go out and hustle this idea," I said.

"I think someone should concentrate on selling to staff," Drew suggested.

"Plus hitting up all our friends and family and neighbors," someone else said.

"What if we make it really fun by dressing up the contestants in slings, splints, casts, that sort of thing?" Chris asked.

"That's good," Miss Piaget said enthusiastically. "Every team should have two members, the pusher and the patient."

"The trick is to get a light patient and a strong pusher," Wendy said.

"We'll really have to practice," I told them. "You can be sure the orderlies will pick Otto for their team."

"He's big, but I bet he's not that fast," Drew said.

"I bet you're right," Chris agreed.

"Okay. Then it's all set. Chris will order the tickets, and we'll all be members of the sales force."

"What about advertising?" Miss Piaget suggested.

"Who's artistic?" I asked, scanning the sea of faces.

The dark-haired girl, whose name I learned was Beverly, raised her hand. "I can't draw," she said, "but I'd be willing to write some news blurbs and submit them around town."

"Terrific."

"I'll do the posters," Wendy volunteered. "It'll be fun."

"Anything else?" The class seemed so excited about my idea.

"I hate to break this up," Miss Piaget said, looking at the clock, "but we have to head for our stations now. Let's get a sign-up sheet going first, though. Everyone put down a phone number where you can be reached. That way we won't have to take any more class time for this. All right, class dismissed. Let's meet back here for a few minutes after rounds," she said, "to finish up on this."

Much to my amazement, nobody groaned. Drew and I walked out of class together. "You know," I said to him, "Miss Piaget isn't so bad after all. At least she hasn't tried to strangle any students with her whistle."

Drew laughed. "See you after rounds," he said, and kissed me lightly on the nose.

*   *   *

I couldn't wait to share the wheelchair race idea with my family. At dinner that night, I told them.

"Sounds like fun, Jordan," Mom said, passing the salad to me.

"Who's going to be on your team?" Jimmy wanted to know.

"We haven't decided that yet, but I'm sure Drew will be the pusher person because he's faster than the rest of us. I guess we'll just draw straws for the honor of being the patient."

"I think being the patient would be fun," Jessica said, biting into her French bread and dropping crumbs all over her lap.

"I don't," Mom disagreed. "What if the wheelchair tipped over? Jessica, move your chair closer to the table, sweetheart."

"If the wheelchair tipped over, then you could be a *real* patient," Jimmy said.

"Boy, wouldn't that be fun," Dad joked sarcastically.

"So how many tickets can I sell you?" I asked innocently.

"What timing you have," Mom said, smiling at me. "Just like your father."

Dad beamed at me proudly. "You can sell us four, sweetie," he said. "And maybe I'll even take some to work with me. Goodness knows I've bought enough peanuts and cookies from everyone else over the years. Now it's turn-around time."

"Gee, thanks, Dad." I turned my attention to my dinner. "Good macaroni, Mom," I told her.

"I'd rather have fried chicken," Jimmy said, twirling his fork in his noodles.

"You *always* want fried chicken," Jessica complained.

He took a bite and said defensively, "Well, so what? Fried chicken is good for you."

"Don't talk with your mouth full," Jessica said in her bossiest voice.

Jimmy pretended to ignore her, and then when Mom and Dad weren't looking, he stuck out his tongue.

"Yuck!" Jessica said. "Don't be gross, Jimmy. Mother, Jimmy's being gross."

"Don't be gross, Jimmy," Mom said automatically.

"Pass the bread, please," Dad requested.

Jimmy stuck out his tongue a second time.

"*Mo-ther!*" Jessica wailed.

*   *   *

It was all decided. The class had voted unanimously that I should be Drew's patient. "Don't you think we should practice?" he asked me.

I gave him a tentative smile. "Right now?"

"We need to get started perfecting our technique," he said seriously. "Get all the bugs out."

"All right," I agreed. "Might as well get used to it now. What will we do for a wheelchair?"

Drew opened the trunk of his car, revealing a folded wheelchair. "On loan from Miss Piaget," he explained.

"You're kidding," I said. "She must really want us to win."

"I think she does. Where to, patient?"

"Might as well go to the scene of the crime," I said.

Drew drove to Sycamore Creek Park. Dusk was upon us and most of the Sunday afternoon picnickers were packing up when we pulled into a parking spot underneath one of the large trees that had given the park its name.

"There are still so many people here," I said anxiously. "I don't want anyone to see us practicing, Drew. It will give it all away."

"Well, let's walk down to the creek then. In another

fifteen or twenty minutes most of the crowd will have cleared out.'' He took my hand and led me down the winding dirt path to the creek. It gurgled and bubbled over the smooth granite stones.

''I used to come here a lot when I was a kid,'' he said, sitting down. ''We lived just two blocks over.'' I sat down next to him. We took off our shoes and dangled our feet in the stream.

''Oh, it's so cold,'' I said.

Drew stood up and pulled me up after him. We waded in the creek. ''There're some tadpoles down here,'' he said. We inspected the tiny creatures. ''Look,'' he continued, ''this one's already a full-fledged frog.'' The big-eyed creature tried to hide under a leaf.

''I hope he eats lots of mosquitoes,'' I said. ''Isn't that watercress?'' I asked, pointing to a small green plant growing in the streambed. ''It has a real peppery taste.''

''Well, I'm not tasting it,'' he said adamantly.

''Why not?'' I asked. ''Watercress is good.''

''I make it a habit never to dine with frogs,'' he said.

I giggled and reached down to pick a small piece. I inspected it carefully and said, ''It's clean enough.'' Then I took a tiny bite of it. ''I was right! It *is* watercress.''

''Terrific, my lady. Now I know just where to come for the ingredients to prepare you elegant crustless sandwiches.''

''I only eat them with caviar,'' I told him, laughing. Then I noticed it was getting really dark. ''We'd better start practicing,'' I said.

''We shouldn't have too many curious onlookers now.''

We waded back up the creek to our shoes and put them on. By the time we reached the parking lot, everyone had gone.

Drew opened the trunk and pulled out the wheelchair.

He unfolded it, then patted the seat. "Ready, my dear?"

I sat down. "I've always wondered what the world looked like from here. We're so lucky not to be stuck in one of these for real," I said, thinking of Susie.

"Don't I know it," he said.

"Onward, James," I commanded, and he pushed me slowly to one end of the parking lot.

"Ready?" he asked.

"I guess so," I said a bit nervously.

"Hang on."

"Wait a minute. How fast are we going to go?"

"As fast as we can, you sissy. Do you want to win this race or not?"

"I'm not sure," I said.

"Well, I am. Put your feet on the foot rests. On your mark . . . get set . . . Drew crouched down behind me, seeking a foothold.

"Go!" I yelled.

He pushed off and started running. At first I was so scared I closed my eyes. When I opened them, we were heading straight for a trash can.

"Turn!" I screamed. "Turn or stop!"

"Where are the brakes?" he yelled back to me, still running along behind.

"What brakes?" I squealed. And then, in the dimming light, I saw it. "Drew, Drew," I pleaded. "Watch out! A bump!"

Too late. He swerved to the right to avoid the bump, and almost tipped me over. To slow us down a little Drew pushed the wheelchair up over the bump and onto the grass. That was a big mistake, for now we were heading downhill, straight for the creek.

"Drew! Drew!" I screamed.

I could feel him pulling backward, but he wasn't strong

enough to overcome the momentum. "I can't stop it, Jordan!"

"I know that!" I screamed again.

"Bail out!" he yelled at me.

"I can't!"

And then suddenly, I was thrust forward. The next thing I knew, I was sprawled out in the shallow water, the wheelchair upside down next to me, the wheels still spinning.

"Are you all right, Jordan?" Drew asked me cautiously.

"I . . . I . . . I think so," I told him.

And then a towering figure was standing over us. A huge fat woman was yelling at Drew: "Young man, that was the cruelest stunt I have ever witnessed." She cooed to me and pulled me from the creek. "Are you all right, sweetheart?"

"I'm fine," I said. "Thank you."

She stood with her hands on her hips and glared at Drew. "That was a horrible trick to pull on your sister."

"But she isn't my sister," Drew said.

"Then that's even worse," the woman continued. "Animosities often develop between siblings, but to deliberately do something like this to a friend . . . a helpless friend."

"I'm not helpless," I told her. "Really. We were just practicing."

"You were practicing being helpless? That's disgusting." She surveyed the two of us. "You should be ashamed of yourselves," she said, "fooling people like that." She wiped her wet hands on her dress and stomped off.

Drew and I watched her until she disappeared beyond the rise. Then we both collapsed on the grass. I could hardly speak, I was laughing so hard. "Is that the lady who had the appendectomy?" I asked.

Drew laughed harder. He pulled the wheelchair from the creek and uprighted it.

"Gosh, I hope we didn't do any permanent damage." I wiped the tears from my eyes. "I haven't laughed so hard in ages."

"Me neither." He inspected the chair. "No problems with this," he said. "Get back in," he directed, "and I'll push you up the hill."

"Forget it," I told him. "I'm not getting back into that thing until the race. No more practicing for me."

"Well, okay. I think the trick is that you have to navigate and I have to steer."

"It's hard to navigate with your eyes closed," I told him.

"Well, keep them open." We started to laugh again.

"Four hundred and twenty-three," I said.

"Four hundred and twenty-three what?" he asked.

"Stitches. Internal and external."

Drew cracked up. "Jordan," he said, "even if we don't win the race, we'll still have the most fun." He leaned over and kissed me tenderly.

Together we pushed the wheelchair back to the car.

Chapter Sixteen

With final exams coming up, both in school and in ROP, I saw very little of Drew. We studied together a little for the hospital test, but he had a lot of tough classes I couldn't help him with at all, like Calculus and French.

Carrie's parents went out of town for a few days, so I spent one night at her house and we studied together for Spanish. She's hopeless in that class. I guess some people just have a knack for languages and some people have a knack for . . . ?

"Carrie, what do you have a knack for?"

"Noise," she said. "Art maybe. Why?" She had her nose in her Spanish book, but I could tell the material wasn't settling in.

"Because they say everyone has a knack for something. I'm pretty good with languages."

"I know. How about taking my final for me?" I shook my head. "I guess I have a knack for fixing things," she said. "I'm pretty good at that. I think I'd make a good grease monkey."

*　　*　　*

As it turned out, Carrie's knack for fixing things came in handy later that evening when I dropped Drew's necklace down the shower drain. I had forgotten to take it off, and I was washing my hair when I felt the heart drop away from my neck. I groped for the chain with my toes while I rinsed the shampoo from my hair and eyes. But by the time I was finally able to see, the necklace had disappeared.

"Carrie!" I screamed. "Carrie! Come here!"

She rushed into the bathroom. "What's wrong, Jordan? What's the matter?"

I was crying now. The towel I had wrapped around me kept coming undone. "I lost my necklace down the drain!"

"That's all? I thought you were having a heart attack. Or Otto was leering in the window. Don't ever scream like that again unless it's an emergency. You scared me to death."

"It *is* an emergency!" I wailed. "I lost my heart!"

"You've lost your head," she said. "Move over. Maybe I can get it." She fiddled with the tub drain and finally pulled part of it free. I tried peering down the dark abyss.

"Jordan, you're dripping all over me!"

I started to cry. "It's gone. How will I ever tell Drew?"

"Quit blubbering. We can get it, I think, but it will mean getting very dirty. We have to crawl under the house."

"What for?"

"Why do you think? To get to the trap."

"But aren't there bugs and spiders and rats under there?"

Carrie stood with her hands on her hips. "Look," she

said, disgusted, ''do you want your necklace or not?''

*   *   *

I put on my jeans and sweat shirt, and together we crawled under the house. ''Couldn't someone else do this?'' I asked. ''I feel like a lizard under here.''

''Who do you suggest?'' Carrie asked, crawling on her belly toward some pipes. ''Shine the light this way.''

I did as I was told.

''And hand me the pipe wrench.''

''Which one is that?''

''The one that isn't the hammer.''

''Oh.'' I could taste the damp dirt in my mouth. ''I just washed my hair,'' I complained. It was a good thing Carrie couldn't reach me easily. At that point I think she might have hit me.

''You think *I* like it under here, Jordan? Is that what you think? Shine the light more to the right.''

As I did so, the beam caught a furry little creature as it scampered under a two by four. ''Carrie, wasn't that a rat?'' I shrieked.

''No. It was a mouse. A tiny mouse.''

I couldn't help whimpering. ''What if it has rabies?''

Carrie ignored me. ''This is the trap, I think.'' She turned over on her back and worked the pipes with the wrench. ''It's loosening,'' she said finally.

Drips fell steadily on her chest. Then the pipe came loose with a loud *thunk!* and water gushed everywhere. All over Carrie, all over the dirt, probably all over the mouse.

She screamed and sat up quickly, bumping her head. I could hear her muttering under her breath. She reached for the valve and turned. The water slowed to a continuous drip.

"I think you're supposed to turn that *before* you take the pipe off," I volunteered. I couldn't see her face well in the darkness, but then, I didn't have to.

"I found the necklace," she said finally. "A few more twists with the wrench and we'll be ready to get out of here."

We removed our filthy clothes in the laundry room in silence. Carrie was no longer speaking to me. *I* had my necklace, but she had a big red goose egg on her forehead.

"Boy, it's a good thing your parents weren't home," I said.

No answer.

I tried again. "I think ROP has a plumber's helper course," I told her. "You'd be a natural, Carrie."

She still wouldn't say anything.

"You were right," I went on. "Absolutely right. You certainly do have a knack for fixing things."

*   *   *

My nurse's aide test was tough. Tougher than I'd ever expected. And Miss Piaget spent the whole hour on patrol, marching up and down the aisles and peering at our answers. It made me very nervous.

"As an aide, what are the three most important qualities you will bring to nursing your patients?" I couldn't think of a single one. I looked over at Drew, who was busy writing. It looked as if one of us was going to pass at least.

I went through the test and answered those questions I was sure of. The others, I left for last. I was working on the seven things a patient may worry about, when Miss

Piaget blew her whistle. "Time's up," she said sternly. "Pass your exams forward."

Well, it was over. At last.

*   *   *

Drew drove me home. "Want to celebrate tonight?"

"Maybe we should wait to see if we passed."

"We passed, Jordan. Don't worry about it." He pulled to a stop in front of my house and leaned over and kissed me. I caught him staring at my necklace. He fiddled with it lightly, then let it fall back against my neck. "Your necklace looks shinier," he said. "Did you clean it or something?"

"Or something," I said. Then I gave him a quick kiss good-bye and jumped out of the car before he could question me further. "Why don't you come over tonight?" I said through the window. "We can make pizzas."

"Sounds like fun," he said.

"And we'll plan the ROP certification party."

Chapter Seventeen

"Jordan, telephone."

"Thanks, Mom." I picked up the phone expecting to hear Pam or Carrie or maybe even Drew, but instead Miss Piaget was on the line.

"Hello, Jordan."

"Miss Piaget. Is the race still on for Saturday?"

"Well, yes, but there's been a slight change in plans."

"What's that?" I asked.

"Well, it seems the hospital is covered insurance-wise only if we have the race on the premises, so I think we should hold it in the garden. It will be safer to push the chairs on the lawn. That pavement could have been potentially dangerous." (How well I knew.) "And this way some of the hospital patients will have an opportunity to witness the festivities. I'd like you to call the others if you would and tell them about the change in plans."

"I'd be happy to. I hope in all the confusion we don't lose any observers."

"We'll put a blurb in Thursday's paper mentioning the

change. And if we post a sign at the park, that should take care of it.''

''I hope so.''

''ROP is counting on you and Drew to win the race for us.''

''We'll do our best. That's all I can promise.''

''That's all we ask. Good-bye, Jordan.''

''Bye, Miss Piaget.''

*   *   *

The race was scheduled for noon. By eleven-thirty the crowds had begun to gather and the wheelchairs were being rolled into position. A special corner of the flower garden had been roped off as a spectators' gallery for those patients well enough to attend the event.

Drew and I had separated to take care of last-minute details, so I was surprised when he tapped me on the shoulder, frowning. I could tell something was bothering him.

''What's wrong?'' I asked.

''Have you looked at the grass?''

''Not closely.''

''Well, I have. It's soaking wet. Apparently no one bothered to mention our race to the gardener, and he left the sprinklers on all night.''

''Oh no. Pretty squishy, huh?''

''It's worse than that. It's like the Florida Everglades.''

''What will we do?''

''Our very best, Jordan. What else can we do?''

I walked over to the grass and stepped on it cautiously. ''Oh my gosh. We'll sink to China.''

''Well, it could be worse. At least you're light.''

By twelve noon all the contestants were gathered at the

starting line. The nurses were represented by Mrs. Dobrowski and Mrs. Chan. Mrs. Dobrowski is head of student nurses and Mrs. Chan is on the pediatrics ward and a real favorite with all the kids. Otto and Bill Helms were representing the orderlies. Bill is a small guy, and just as Drew had guessed, he manned the "patient" position while Otto stood behind the wheels. Two young doctors I didn't recognize completed the field.

"Looks like some stiff competition," I whispered to Drew.

He squeezed my hand. "We'll do fine," he whispered back.

The superintendent of the hospital, Mr. Forde, described the course. "Entrants," he explained, "you will race your chairs around the flower garden, past the fish pond, and down to the street, where you will turn around and return to the starting line."

"To the street and back?" I squawked to Drew. "That means part of the race is uphill!"

"The only rule," Mr. Forde continued, "is that there can be no substitutions. The same two entrants who begin the race must finish it. Any questions?"

No one said anything.

"Then, contestants ready?" he asked.

That was my cue to position myself in the wheelchair. The other "patients" did likewise. A cheer went up from the crowd as we were introduced. Carrie, Pam, and my family led the ROP cheering section.

"Good luck and may the best team win!" Mr. Forde shouted. "On your mark, get set . . . *go!*"

We were off. Or I thought we were off. Drew found pushing the chair on the wet grass almost impossible. "Hurry!" I screamed. "The orderlies are getting ahead of us!"

With Otto's great strength, I could see that his team would have little trouble winning the race. But Drew wasn't about to give up, and he continued to push as hard as he could. Mud flew everywhere. Soon my white nurse's uniform was covered with brown spatters. Our wheels dug into the grass.

"Keep going, Drew!" I shouted to him. "Keep going!"

"Jordan, hold still!" he yelled back. We were gaining, actually gaining on Otto.

I yelled to the other team, "Look out, orderlies, here we come!"

As Otto looked back over his shoulder to check the distance, his legs went out from under him and he sprawled helplessly in the mud. I swear I saw him bounce. I couldn't help laughing. Bill looked frantic. "They're taking the lead!" I heard Otto yell. Hurry, Bill! Help me up!"

I turned back to watch Otto regain his balance. He was limping. Bill and Otto argued loudly with each other and then Otto took the "patient" position.

"We've got it now!" I yelled to Drew.

We left the nurses far behind, convulsed in a state of hysterical laughter. They couldn't seem to get their chair beyond the first rise. The doctors turned the wrong way at the flower garden and had to start over.

The cheers from the crowd spurred us on. "Come on, ROP," Dad yelled. "You can do it!"

All of a sudden our right wheel caught in the mud and I was thrown clear of the chair when Drew tried to negotiate a turn. "Get back in!" he demanded, yanking me from the wet grass and rudely plunking me back into the chair.

"Is that any way to treat your patient?" I screamed at him.

"Look!" he yelled. "They've passed us!"

Sure enough, on the downhill, Otto and Bill had managed to overtake us. "While you were busy rolling around in the mud," Drew screamed, "they caught up!" He went even faster, once again almost dumping his precious cargo to the ground.

At the turnaround point, we were in second place. "Here comes the hard part," I screeched to Drew.

"Not hard for you," he complained, pushing me up the hill. And that's where we got lucky. As Bill attempted to push Otto up the hill, he actually lost ground. We almost collided with the doctors' team barreling down the lawn toward us.

"Look out!" I shrieked at them. The nurses were still laughing and rolling around on the wet grass, unable to participate because they were giggling so hard.

I took one look back at our only real adversaries. As I did so, Otto's wheelchair rolled backward, dumping both its occupant and its trusty hanger-on into the fish pond. The crowd roared. I heard Otto roar too.

Drew slowed down. I could tell he was exhausted. Once again I turned around. Much to my surprise, I saw that the doctors were gaining on us. "Faster, Drew. Faster! They're catching up!"

At the top of the rise we were neck and neck, but then Drew really poured on the steam. I crouched down in the chair, trying to lower the wind resistance. "Run, Drew!" someone cried. "Run!"

He gave it his best. Which was just good enough. We crossed the finish line two seconds ahead of the doctors. A cheer went up from the crowd, and then before I could get out of the seat I was surrounded by happy well-wishers. Now I know how Miss America feels when she gets mobbed by all those huggy-kissy females.

The pandemonium continued for a few more minutes until Superintendent Forde took the podium once again. "Ladies and gentlemen," he yelled. "May I have your attention please?"

The crowd quieted. "We have to announce our winners. Would you come up here, please?" he said, beckoning to Drew and me. My knees felt rubbery, both from exhaustion and delight as I climbed the two steps to the small stage.

"Congratulations," the superintendent said. "On behalf of West Valley Hospital, it gives me great pleasure to crown you the winners of our first wheelchair race. I think it should be an annual event, folks; don't you?"

An affirmative cheer erupted from the crowd. He asked us our names. "Miss Jordan Collins," he said with feigned formality, "I crown you top charioteer." He slipped a laurel-leaf wreath—made entirely of Band-Aids—over my head. He repeated the process for Drew. My crown kept slipping down over one eye, which gave the gathered audience a good laugh.

Miss Piaget came up on stage. "I would just like to thank a terrific bunch of kids," she said. "The proceeds from this fund-raiser will be used to purchase music equipment for the hospital's sun room."

Everyone applauded.

"I also have an award for the winning team," she continued, handing Drew a package which he quickly tore open.

"Oh boy! Just what we needed!" He laughed and held up the gift for everyone to see. "A year's supply of tongue depressors. How depressing," he punned.

The crowd chuckled.

Miss Piaget said loudly, "I'd also like to thank the entire West Valley staff for being such an incredible group

to work with. You've made our time here fun. Thanks.''
She waved to the crowd and quickly left the stage.

Drew and I started to step down, too, but we were
detained by Mr. Forde. "I have another little surprise for
you," he said. "Mel's Sporting Goods Store has gra-
ciously donated a gift certificate to the winners." He
handed it to Drew. "Congratulations, once again," he
said, shaking Drew's hand and kissing me on the cheek.

And then, as quickly as it began, the event was over.
Tired, but happy, I watched the crowd disperse. Orderlies
and nurses wheeled the patients back to their rooms. Some
of the ROP class took our "chariots" away to be cleaned
up.

I surveyed the lawn, which was a real mess. "That was
fun," I told Drew. "But we're going to have to volunteer
our time to repair the grass."

"It *was* fun. I bet if we practiced regularly, we could
become unbeatable. World champions."

"Don't let one victory go to your head," I warned him.

Mom and Dad came over to congratulate us. So did
Drew's parents. He introduced me. It was embarrassing,
shaking hands with them while I was covered in mud, but
they didn't seem to mind. In fact, they laughed and joked
with me and made me feel less awkward.

"Need a ride home?" Drew asked.

"I think I'll go home with my folks, if you don't mind. I
wouldn't want to spread all this good earth around in
anyone else's car."

"Okay if I pick you up about three? We could go over
and pick out our prize at Mel's."

"I'd love it," I told him.

"See you at three then," he said, squeezing my hand.

*   *   *

Dad put his arm around my shoulder and we walked to our car. Jessica and Jimmy chattered non-stop. "Was it fun?" Jimmy asked, walking backward and almost bumping into a tree. Mom yanked him out of the way. "It looked like fun."

I nodded.

"That was so silly when those two guys fell in the fish pond," Jessica said.

"I'm just happy we earned enough to buy the stereo," I told my family.

"The race was a great idea, Jordan," Mom said. "And I think everyone had a good time. I know I did."

"I did too, Mom. Except this mud is starting to feel very uncomfortable."

"You had a mud bath," Dad joked. "They're supposed to be very healthy."

"But they're not very clean," Jessica said, laughing.

We saw Otto in the parking lot. He was still soaking wet.

"I hope you weren't hurt," I said to him.

He smiled. "Nah, and I needed a bath anyway." He waved to us. I noticed, though, that he seemed to be favoring one leg a little. Poor Otto.

Carrie and Pam were waiting for us at the car. "Oh, Jordan," Carrie squealed. "That was terrific! I knew you could do it." She squeezed me tightly, apparently not minding the dirt.

"Watch out for my crown," I told her.

"You girls need a ride home?" Dad asked.

"No, thanks. We rode our bikes," Pam said. "They're around the building. Well, see ya, Jordan."

"Okay," I said. "See you. And thanks for the support. I could hear you cheering us on all the way."

"Well, what are friends for?" Carrie asked, wide-eyed. She and Pam waved good-bye and headed for their bikes.

When I got home I hung my Band-Aid wreath right next to my severed fan belt. The interesting combination made me smile every time it caught my eye.

Chapter Eighteen

By the time Drew arrived, I had showered and cleaned off the mud and grass stains. "Well, winner, are you ready to pick out your prize?" he said.

"I'm ready," I said. "How much money do we have?"

Drew pulled an envelope out of his pocket and showed it to me. "The certificate is worth fifteen dollars."

"What can we buy with that?"

"That's what we're going to find out. Let's go take a look."

We drove to the far end of town where Mel's Sporting Goods Store is situated next to a used car lot. We parked the car and Drew led me by the hand into the store.

"What should we look at first?" I asked.

"Well, we can rule out ski stuff, unless you just want a hat. We couldn't even buy one glove with what we won. Besides, summer's almost here, so let's concentrate on summer stuff. Do you like to fish?"

"I like to eat fish," I said, "but I've never caught one.

121

Except in our aquarium, with the net. But I don't think that counts.''

''You're right. It doesn't.''

Drew and I walked down the aisle that held the tackle boxes, the fishing poles, and the lures. ''I never knew there were so many different ways to catch a fish,'' I said. ''Hey! How about these?'' I wandered over to a large pair of rubber pants with boots attached that almost stood up by themselves.

''Those are called waders, Jordan. Fishermen use them to wade in the streams so they can get closer to their catch.''

I slipped out of my sandals and looked around. The store was busy and no one seemed to be paying much attention to us. I stepped into the waders and pulled the suspenders up over my shoulders. ''Well, what do you think?'' I asked.

''They look a little big,'' Drew said, laughing.

''A little? I think they were made for a giant.'' I took a step and almost fell over.

''May I help you?'' a stern voice from behind me said.

''Ah, we were just looking for some waders for my father,'' Drew explained to the salesman, looking very sheepish and giving me a ''get out of those things *now*'' glance. I did, though rather awkwardly. ''But we think these are too much money,'' he added quickly.

''Well, let me know if I can be of any assistance,'' the man said. He had white hair and wore a bow tie. ''We're willing to help you, but we don't like kids fooling around with the merchandise.''

''That's very understandable, sir,'' Drew said, yanking me by the hand down the aisle. ''Did you have to get into those things?'' he asked me. ''You almost got us thrown out of here, and we haven't decided on our prize yet.''

Then he laughed. "You did look pretty silly in those," he said.

We wandered up and down the aisle that held all the fishing poles. "How do these work?" I asked Drew. Before he could answer, I had picked up a pole and released some of the line. I tossed it back behind me, the way I'd seen the fishermen on the pier do it. When I pulled forward again, the line was taut. The look on Drew's face told me I had hooked a big one.

His face turned white. "Uh-oh," he said.

I heard the voice before I saw the face. "I thought I told you kids to ask for assistance," the same grumpy salesman said, disentangling the fishing line from his bow tie.

Drew came to my rescue. "You should never have a hook on a display pole," he told the man sternly. "That's very dangerous. Someone could get hurt. And Mel's could get sued." Once again he grabbed my hand and yanked me to safety.

"That line sure tangles easily," I told Drew. He ignored my remark and dragged me over to look at all the camping equipment.

"How about a sleeping bag, Jordan? We could share it."

"Oh, really?" I asked.

Drew looked sort of flustered. "I didn't mean like that. I meant we could take turns."

I looked at the price. "Not enough money."

"Well, what's left?" he asked. We tried on waterskis and pulled each other along on the carpet, all the while mindful of the fact that Mr. Grump could show up at any minute. We crawled inside a pup tent and it immediately collapsed. I couldn't help giggling. Fortunately, our grouchy salesman was busy with a customer in another part of the store when we crawled out.

Drew introduced me to the wonders of camping economy. The little mess kits with their miniature cookware were totally amazing. "They're so tiny and cute," I said, dismantling one. "Now how do they fit back together?"

It took the two of us fifteen minutes to figure out the intricacies of the mess-kit puzzle, and when we were done, we were left with one tiny tin cup that for some reason just wouldn't cooperate and collapse. "I give up," I said and stuck the cup in a port-a-potty. Luckily, Mr. Grump was busy putting the pup tent back up.

"Careful," Drew whispered to me. "He's just one step behind us."

Drew tried on a snorkel, mask, and flippers. I had to laugh because he looked like some monster from the blue lagoon. I sprayed him with insect repellent and when he put a hunter's orange cap on his head, I giggled—he looked so funny.

I tried on a camouflage outfit and wandered around the store incognito. Every time anyone looked at me, I held real still and pretended I was a mannequin.

Finally Drew said, "Come on, we don't have all day for this. Let's find something."

We looked at weights and barbells. I rode two miles on the stationary bicycle, and Drew bounced on the miniature trampoline almost to the ceiling and back.

Some funny-looking boot caught his attention. "Oh, neat, Jordan," he said. "Gravitational boots." He put them on and hung himself from a bar.

"Are you crazy?" I whispered to him. I had to bend over almost to the ground so he could hear me. "You're going to get us thrown out of here!"

"I can't hear you, Jordan," he said. "Bend down lower."

I bent over farther, but Drew's head was swinging back and forth about three inches from the floor. "If you fall, you'll kill yourself," I said.

"This is fun," he told me, "except all the blood is rushing to my head."

"And Mr. Grump is rushing over here. What do you expect upside down?"

"Are you interested in our gravitational boots?" a masculine voice boomed. I knew it. Caught in the act. Again.

"Depends on how much they are," Drew said, pulling himself up and disconnecting his feet from the contraption.

"They're more than fifteen dollars," I whispered to him, tugging on his arm.

"Seventy-five dollars," our salesman said sternly.

"Oh," Drew responded cheerfully. "Then we're not interested. Maybe we'll come back when they're on sale."

"They *are* on sale," the old man muttered. "Look, I'm afraid I'm going to have to ask you two to—"

Drew pulled the certificate from his pocket. "We were given this as a gift," he interrupted. "We haven't decided yet what we want." For the third time he grabbed my hand. "I think we'll just sort of mosey around and see if we can't find something."

"Just don't try anything on," the salesman warned.

I looked at my watch. We had been in the store almost an hour. "Did you notice how red that salesman's face was getting?" I asked Drew.

"Yeah, I don't understand it," he said. "I was the one who was upside down."

"I think we were upsetting him, Drew. Maybe we should come back some other time."

"Nah. We'll find something. Come on."

We looked at volleyballs, tennis balls, basketballs. "I could use a new tennis racket," Drew said, inspecting several carefully. "But they're too expensive."

"Well, what about a badminton racket. They're cheaper. And it's a fun game." I swatted at a birdie and it flew skyward and landed in the fluorescent light fixture. Fortunately, no one noticed. At least they didn't notice what caused the bulb to start flickering erratically. We left that aisle quickly before we could be accused of sabotaging the store.

"I think we should just leave," I told Drew.

"Maybe you're right," he said.

It was then that I noticed the inflatable rafts. "Look, Drew, aren't they neat? They even have tiny little oars."

We walked over to the display and studied the rafts carefully.

"Wow," Drew said. "Some of these even have available outboard motors. They're really something. They'd be great for fishing."

"It would sure take a lot of air to pump them up," I said, thinking of the hard time I had at the beach just blowing up the twins' inner tubes.

"Nah, it's not hard," Drew explained. "You just step on this inflation pedal. It does it for you."

"What inflation pedal?" I asked.

"Right here. It's simple."

I put my foot down squarely on the pedal as Drew directed. All of a sudden, the raft started unfolding, inflating. It seemed as though it was expanding to yacht size.

Tiny children shrieked, teenagers giggled, and the salesman with the bow tie came running toward us. His eyes were bulging and his face had turned purple.

"I think we'd better leave," I suggested to Drew.

"I think maybe you're right," he agreed.

"*Out!*" The old man bellowed, pointing an accusing finger at us. "*Out! Now!*"

I'm not sure if it was the salesman's lack of control or what, but suddenly Drew managed to compose himself. I was ready to run, but Drew calmly pulled the certificate from his pocket once again and handed it to the hysterical man. "We'd just like our money please."

Mr. Grump grabbed the certificate and stared at it. "You ruined this store for fifteen dollars?" he said. Then he walked over to the cash register and pushed a button. A bell rang and the drawer clanged open. He quickly handed Drew a ten and a five.

"I wonder if that was Mel, the owner," I asked Drew as we were walking back to the car.

"I don't know," he said. "Maybe. He sure was grouchy, though."

"Yeah, I know," I answered him. "I just don't understand it."

"Me either. But come on. With fifteen bucks we can buy a couple of hamburgers plus two hot-fudge sundaes."

Chapter Nineteen

Just my luck. Drew asked me to go miniature golfing with him this weekend, almost my favorite thing in the entire world, and I can't go. "Drew!" I complained. "I don't believe this. Not five minutes ago I accepted a baby-sitting job for Friday night."

"Well, I didn't know until five minutes ago that I didn't have to work at the shop. Now I guess I will work."

"Talk about poor timing."

"Yeah. Oh well. We'll do it some other time. Where are you working?"

"Down the street at the Reeveses'. Do you know them?"

"Don't think so," he said.

"They live in that little colonial on the corner," I told him.

"Okay. I know the place."

"They have two cute kids, two and four."

"Maybe I could come over and help you?" he asked hopefully.

"I wouldn't care, and I bet even the Reeveses wouldn't mind, but I don't think Mom would like it."

"Well, I'll call you then, okay? There's no harm in that. Maybe we can play gin rummy over the telephone."

"Even over the phone I'll still beat you."

"That's only because I won't be able to see your cards."

"Are you accusing me of cheating?"

"The idea never crossed my mind, my dear."

"I bet. Well, anyway, you could call and serenade me with your terrific voice, or tell me jokes or something."

"Deal," he said. "I'll practice until then."

*   *   *

Friday night at six o'clock I arrived at the Reeveses'. They were going out for dinner with some friends and then to a movie.

"We should be back around eleven, eleven-thirty, Jordan," Mrs. Reeves said. "The emergency numbers are all on the wall next to the telephone. Oh, and would you mind feeding Candy and Derek their dinners for me? They wanted to wait for you. The food is warming in the oven."

"No problem, Mrs. Reeves." I lifted Candy into her high chair and reached for her bib. "You look very pretty tonight," I told Mrs. Reeves.

Mr. Reeves kissed his wife. "I think she does too," he said, grinning at me.

The Reeveses have the kind of house I would like to have someday. Mrs. Reeves has picked all warm and cozy colors for her furniture. An old quilt hangs on the wall as a piece of artwork. A large basket full of pinecones sits next to the fireplace. The living-room furniture is upholstered in green plaid. And Mrs. Reeves always has fresh-cut flowers all over the house, straight from her garden. Tonight she left me a bowl of bright red apples next to the television as a treat.

"Hungry, Candy?" I asked the big-eyed little girl, tying the bib around her neck. "Let's see what your mom left for dinner."

"She left stew," Derek told me. "With dumplings. I helped her make them yesterday. They're leftovers, but you can have some if you want."

"No thanks, Derek. I've already eaten."

"We have Jell-O too," he informed me. "It's red. Red's my favorite color of Jell-O. Is it yours?"

"Yes," I said. I filled a small bowl with stew and found a spoon for Candy. The baby reached for her food.

"Hold on, shortcake," I said. "I have to cut the meat into small pieces so you can eat it." I filled two glasses with milk and set them in front of the children. Derek hopped off his chair and headed for the refrigerator. "I'm getting the Jell-O," he announced.

The phone rang. "Hi," Carrie said. "Your mom told me you were baby-sitting."

"Hi," I told her. "Can I call you back? I'm right in the middle of feeding the kids, no easy chore."

"Sure. No problem."

"No problem for you," I complained, wiping off the gravy that Candy had splattered on my sleeve.

"Well, no one ever said baby-sitting was easy."

"I just wonder how mothers do it full time. I have more respect for them every time I come over here." There was a crash as Derek dropped the bowl of red Jell-O all over the floor. He started to cry.

"Look, I've really got to go, Carrie. It's clean-up time. Talk to you later."

I soothed Derek's tears, cleaned up the mess on the floor, and managed to locate a can of peaches in the cupboard to act as a substitute dessert. As far as Derek was concerned, they were a poor second to red Jell-O; but Candy ate them with no complaint.

I set the kids in front of the television set to watch a Disney movie while I finished cleaning up the kitchen. "As soon as I'm done in here," I told them, "we'll have a bath, okay?"

"Are you going to have a bath too?" Derek wanted to know. Candy hauled her blanket after her and sucked her thumb.

"No," I said, trying not to laugh. "I've already had mine."

By eight-thirty I had them both washed and tucked into clean pajamas. They were both looking sleepy—Candy kept rubbing her eyes, and Derek yawned repeatedly—by the time I put them to bed. Candy slept in the crib in the corner of their room, and Derek slept in a junior bed on the other side of the window. "They're happier together," Mrs. Reeves had explained to me. "At least at this age."

I kissed them both, gave Derek a glass of water, and turned on the night light. Immediately, Candy started to cry.

"She wants her doggie," Derek explained from his bed.

"What doggie? You don't have a dog."

"Her stuffed doggie," he said. "Muffy. On the rocking chair."

I handed the baby the ratty stuffed animal and she immediately snuggled down in her crib. "You two go to sleep now," I said. "Good night, you monkeys." I closed their door only halfway.

"We're not monkeys," I heard Derek call after me. "*You're* a monkey."

* * *

The phone rang. It was Drew. "How goes it?" he asked.

"I'm exhausted," I said truthfully.

"It's not so easy playing Mommy, is it?"

"Who's playing? Tonight I feel like the real thing."

"I just got off work," he said. "Wish I could come over."

"I wish you could too. But you can't. You were going to sing to me, remember?"

Just then a tiny face peeped around the corner. "What is it, Derek?" I asked, trying to keep my voice even. He was beginning to test my patience.

"Candy's making a funny noise in her mouth," he said.

"Hang on, Drew," I told him. "I have to check on the baby."

I went quickly to the children's room. The first thing I noticed, even in the dim light, was the fact that Candy had a strange look on her face. When I flipped on the light I saw that she was quickly turning a dark shade of red.

"Oh my God!" I grabbed the baby and rushed her into the kitchen. Then I grabbed the telephone. "It's the baby, Drew!" I screamed. "She's choking!"

"Help her, Jordan!" he yelled back at me. "You know how." And then more calmly, "I'll call the paramedics."

Everything I'd learned in nurse's training seemed to fade away. I looked again at Candy, who was now turning blue. Quickly, automatically, I turned her over my knee, so that her head was lower than the rest of her body.

Somewhere in the backround I could hear Derek crying, but I could only deal with one emergency at a time. I rapped Candy four times between the shoulder blades with the heel of my hand. Nothing. I pushed her tiny tummy closer into my knees, putting more force on her abdomen, and repeated the back blows.

Suddenly, a black circular object came flying out of her mouth. It fell to the floor and rolled under the table. Candy immediately started to cry. But now, at least, she seemed to be breathing normally.

I heard the screech of brakes outside, and then the slam of a car door. Someone ran up the walk and pounded on the door. "Paramedics," a male voice yelled. I quickly opened the door to two uniformed men. Behind them I could see Drew get out of his car and run up the front walk.

"She's all right now, I think," I explained to them. "She was choking, but whatever it was came up."

Derek was beside me, pulling on my jeans. "It was Muffy's eye," he said, handing me a round plastic disk. "I crawled under the table to get it for you."

"Thank you, Derek," I told him.

"As long as we're here, we'll check her out," the paramedic said. He tried to take Candy from my arms, but she shrieked when he came near and clung more tightly to me.

"It's okay," the paramedic said in a gentle voice. He took out a stethoscope. "I can listen with you holding her, but from the sound of that cry, I'd say she's going to be just fine. Kids are pretty resilient, you know." When he put the stethoscope to her chest she screamed again and tried to push it away.

"You did a good job, Jordan," Drew said, congratulating me.

"It's funny," I told him, "but all that training did come back to me. I was afraid that in a real emergency I would panic, but I didn't."

"The benefit of all those tedious hours of practice."

The paramedic looked down Candy's throat, and she screamed louder. "Muffy!" she wailed.

Derek brought the stuffed dog to his sister, who immediately reached out for it. But Drew grabbed it first and carefully inspected the toy. Before giving it to Candy, he quietly turned his back and pulled off the dog's other plastic eye.

"We don't need any more of these hanging around," he said.

The paramedic finished his examination. "Is this your sister?" he asked me. I explained that I was just baby-sitting. "You should be proud of yourself," he said. "Quite likely your quick thinking saved this youngster's life. I'm sure she's going to be fine, but to be on the safe side, we'd suggest that the parents take her to their private physician—just as a precautionary measure, you understand."

The other paramedic closed his bag, and then the two of them left. With the strangers gone and her beloved stuffed animal in her tiny hands, Candy immediately calmed down and stopped crying. But now she and Derek looked totally wide-awake.

"Are you sure you can handle this?" Drew asked me.

"No," I said honestly, still a bit shaken from the ordeal. Candy clung to me. "I hate to ruin the Reeveses' evening out, but I guess I'd better call and let them know what happened. Would you mind staying until they get here?"

"Not at all," Drew said. And then to Derek who was

taking this all in, "How about some ice cream, pardner? You don't look too sleepy to me."

*   *   *

When the Reeveses arrived a little more than forty-five minutes later, Candy was still wide-awake, hugging me and Muffy. Derek had drifted back off to sleep in front of the television set.

Candy released her death grip on me only when she saw her mother enter the room. The Reeveses listened quietly while I explained what had happened. And they calmly accepted Drew's being in their home once they understood the circumstances.

"The paramedics are sure Candy is fine," I told them. "But they suggested you take her to your own doctor so he can look her over, just to be sure."

"We don't know how to thank you, Jordan," Mrs. Reeves said, hugging her daughter to her. "You certainly acted quickly."

"I was just glad I'd had the training so I knew exactly what to do," I said sincerely.

"From now on, you're number one on our baby-sitting list."

"Thanks, Mr. Reeves. And I'm sorry about your evening."

"Don't be sorry," he said. "We had a marvelous dinner and the movie struck me as overrated anyway. At least what we saw of it. It didn't look as though we were going to be missing much. Besides," he added softly, gazing at his baby, "the most important things are right here in this room. We are just so grateful that you knew what to do. Do you need a ride home?" he asked.

Drew quickly intervened. "I can take her home, Mr. Reeves. It's on my way."

Mr. Reeves handed me a twenty-dollar bill. "I don't have any change," I explained to him.

"That's all right," he said. "We want you to keep it. It would be more, but that's all I have on me. It's little enough thanks for what you did."

Suddenly I was embarrassed. I didn't feel comfortable about being paid for doing what I had to do, for doing only what I hoped someone would do for my family in similar circumstances.

"Well, good night," I said to them.

"Bye, bye," Candy said, waving to me.

"I hope Candy doesn't associate me with choking from now on," I told Drew as we walked to his car.

"She probably won't even remember it in the morning," he said, opening the door for me.

"But I will, Drew. It's something I'll remember for a long time. In fact, I don't think I'll ever forget how scary that whole thing was."

*   *   *

We sat out in his car in front of my house and talked for a while. "I was so proud of you tonight," he said.

"You've already said that," I told him.

"Well, I mean it, Jordan. I'm not sure I could have done as well."

"Of course you could have," I told him. "I think instinct or second nature or something just takes over in emergencies."

"I hope I never have to find out. But I'm very thankful to ROP for the opportunity to learn the procedures. And for the opportunity to meet you." He leaned over and kissed me.

"I could stay out here with you forever," I said dreamily, leaning back against the seat of his car and staring out into the dark night. I was finally beginning to relax a bit.

"No, you couldn't," he said.

"Why couldn't I?" I teased. "Trying to get rid of me?"

"Well, for one thing," he said, "your parents would never approve. And for another— Oh my gosh, Jordan," he said, quickly starting the car's engine. "In all the confusion I just rushed out of the house. I didn't even tell my parents where I was going. I've got to get back home." He kissed me once again briefly and scooted me out of the car.

"Good night," I called after him, then watched as he drove away into the darkness.

* * *

Mom and Dad looked terribly anxious as I described Candy's close call. "Thank goodness you were able to help her," Mom said when I'd finished the story. "Otherwise the evening might have been a tragedy." She shuddered at the thought of it. "Why didn't you call us?"

"I didn't have time, Mother. I just did what I had to do."

Dad looked very serious. "Maybe it would be a good thing if the entire family learned some of the emergency procedures you've been taught. We can't always rely on you being around."

"I think that's a wonderful idea," Mom said. "When do we start?"

"Would tomorrow be soon enough?" I asked. "All of a sudden I feel sort of exhausted."

"Understandably so," Mom said. "If you like, I'll make you some hot tea before bed."

"That would be great, Mom," I told her. "With lemon in it?"

"Yes, sweetie. With lemon. Just the way you like it."

* * *

The telephone rang as I was finishing my tea. "Who could that be at this hour?" Mom asked.

"I think I know, Mom," I said, answering the phone.

"I just wanted you to know that everything's okay on this end," Drew said. "When I explained the situation to my folks, they were very understanding."

"I'm glad."

"Me too. Maybe we can go miniature golfing next weekend," he said. "If you're not baby-sitting."

"I think I need a rest from baby-sitting for a while," I told him. "I can't take too much more excitement."

* * *

That night as I snuggled in bed with Julius, I dreamed of children laughing and playing in the park. All healthy children, thank goodness. I guess my experience left me with only positive side effects—especially the knowledge that I can really help another person if necessary. That's a pretty powerful feeling. One to feel good about. Great about, in fact.

Chapter Twenty

"I passed! I passed!" I screamed. I waved the notice in the air and jumped around the room.

"Of course you passed, Jordan," Mom said. "I never doubted that. Here, let me see."

I handed her the letter. "I've got to call Carrie!" I said.

"Jordan Lynn Collins," Mom read aloud. "A *certified* nurse's aide."

"Wow-ee! How 'bout that?" I dialed Carrie's number. "Hi, it's me," I said. "Guess what? I passed my ROP course. Now we can have the party!"

* * *

Mom and Dad went along with the party plans. In fact, they were very helpful organizing the entire thing. We decided on a pot-luck barbecue in our back yard.

Dad and Drew set up the volleyball net, Jessica and Jimmy cleaned off the Ping-Pong table, and Mom helped me decorate everything. We chose red and white—the Red Cross colors—as our theme.

We put red and white checked tablecloths on the picnic and card tables, and we used red and white carnations for centerpieces. Carrie carved a big juicy watermelon into the shape of a basket and filled it with fresh fruit. Mom made a strawberry/ginger ale punch and served it in her big glass bowl.

Drew and Carrie helped me put the last of the silverware on the tables before our guests arrived. "We picked a perfect day for the party," Carrie said.

I knew exactly what she meant. The afternoon was warm and the sky bright and clear.

"You know what we forgot?" Drew said.

I checked the tables over. Plates, silverware, napkins, cups—everything was in place. "What?" I said.

"Music," he told me. "I bet some of the kids would like to dance. I know I would." He winked at me.

"Really? I thought you were only interested in eating."

He quickly swallowed an olive and grinned at me sheepishly. "Well, that too."

"Let me ask Dad if we can bring the stereo outside."

Dad suggested moving the speakers to the other side of the living room so they sat next to the open windows. Carrie went through all my records and pulled out her favorites. "Now if only I had someone to dance with," she said wistfully.

At two o'clock our guests started arriving. Wendy and Chris each brought a huge salad: Wendy's hot German potato smelled wonderful, and Chris's crisp green lettuce leaf looked pretty against the red and white tablecloth.

Miss Piaget brought a crock pot of chili, a distinguished-looking gentleman whom she introduced as a doctor on staff at the hospital, and the dummy Matilda. I guess Miss Piaget really does have a sense of humor. Matilda was the hit of the afternoon.

French bread, baked beans, and a variety of desserts soon filled the tables. Dad started the barbecue and cooked the hamburgers and franks. A delicious aroma filled the air.

"This party was a great idea, Jordan," Drew said. He had his arm around Matilda. "I'd like you to meet my date. Matilda, be a lady and shake hands with Jordan." Matilda just sat there.

"I guess she doesn't like me," I said.

"Nonsense," Drew replied. "She's just shy. Come on, Matilda, how about a dance?" He whirled the dummy around in time to the music until Dad cut in.

Otto arrived late pushing Mr. Harris ahead of him. "Oh, Otto, you brought him. Thank you."

"No problem." Otto looked faintly embarrassed.

"Hungry, Mr. Harris? What can I get for you?" I pushed his wheelchair under a shady tree and went off to fix him a plate.

Just then Carrie came rushing over to me. "That's her!" she whispered excitedly. "The one who was at the dance with Drew!"

Susie and her parents had arrived. "I know, Carrie," I said. "I invited her. Drew and I have resolved all that, and well . . . Susie's a nice girl. I like her."

It was Susie's parents who really convinced me I had done the right thing. When I introduced myself, they both thanked me profusely for all I'd done for their daughter.

"I haven't done anything," I said.

"We think you have," her father replied. "Susie's really blossomed since her last stay at the hospital. She's become more outgoing, more accepting of things. And she talks all the time about you and that nice young man over there. What's his name? Drew?'' He nodded toward Drew, who was standing a few feet away talking to Miss Piaget.

"She does?"

"Yes. The two of you have been a positive influence for Susie, and we really appreciate it.''

I was astounded. I led Susie's parents to the food and then excused myself. There was something I had to do.

Otto was sitting by himself, eating. I walked over to him and sat down. "Otto?'' I said carefully. "May I join you?''

He swallowed and said politely, "Please do.''

"I'm glad you came, Otto. And that was very sweet of you to bring Mr. Harris. I know that meant a trip for you to the convalescent hospital.''

Otto ate his hamburger.

"Otto, I want you to know that I was wrong about you. And . . . and well, I'm sorry.''

Otto's cheeks bulged and he was unable to say anything.

"I guess you know I was afraid of you.'' I shrugged. "My overactive imagination and all.''

He swallowed. "I know I have that effect on some people. Because I'm so big,'' he said.

"It was wrong of me to behave the way I did toward you. Will you forgive me?''

It was Otto's turn to shrug his shoulders. "Don't worry about it, missy. It's already been forgotten.''

*   *   *

The rest of the party went well. My guests played Ping-Pong and volleyball. They ate dessert. They danced. Drew and I danced, too. It felt good when he held me in his arms.

"Hey," he whispered softly in my ear. "Don't look now, but Carrie has found a partner." Drew swung me around gently. I had to chuckle. Carrie seemed dwarfed by Otto.

"It's funny," I whispered back. "I thought she was afraid of big guys. But it looks as though she's having a good time." And why not? Otto, after all, was no one to fear.

Miss Piaget and her doctor friend were also dancing. They seemed to fit together perfectly. I giggled at that. Obviously, I'd been wrong about Miss Piaget, too. She did have another life outside the hospital.

By sundown, most of our guests had said their good-byes and left. Otto took Mr. Harris back to the convalescent hospital and Miss Piaget took Matilda back to her cupboard.

Drew, Carrie, and I were cleaning up the patio when Pam stopped by with Don and his cousin Willy. There were enough leftovers to feed the three of them. I noticed Carrie didn't seem terrified of Don's cousin, but I agreed with her; he sure was big.

"Jordan," Carrie said, "did you know your name was in the paper? Yours too, Drew. Otto told me. There's a whole article on the ROP nurse's aide program."

"Gee," I said. "Lucky me. Maybe some of the four hundred and eighty-two members of my class will see it. But if not, it's okay. They'll remember my name when they come to me for major surgery."

"Nurses don't do surgery," Drew said.

"So who said I was going to be a nurse?" I told him. "I may have bigger plans," I said, teasingly.

"We brought our dance pictures to show you," Pam said. She pulled open her purse and handed me a photo.

"You look beautiful in that dress, Pam," I told her, and really meant it.

Willy reached inside his coat pocket and withdrew his picture. "Here's ours, Carrie," he said, and gave it to her.

"Where's yours?" I asked Drew quietly.

"I gave it to Susie." I fought back a tiny twinge of jealousy. But it didn't last. Susie could have the picture. *I* had Drew.

"What are your plans for the summer, Willy?" I asked.

He looked shyly over at Carrie, then back to me. "Oh, I'll probably just hang around the beach as much as possible."

"Carrie's a good swimmer," I said quickly, glad at last for the opportunity to get back at her. It worked. She blushed crimson. "And she *loves* the beach," I added.

"That's good," Willy said. "Maybe we can all go together."

"I have to get a job," Pam complained. "Dad says I have to pay at least part of my car insurance."

"I'll ask at the market for you if they have any openings," Willy said, "but I wouldn't count on it. You're going to have a tough time finding work at this late date."

"Don't I know it," Pam said glumly.

"What about you, Jordan? What are your plans?" Don asked.

"Baby-sitting, some housework for the neighbors, whatever I can find," I answered. "I've put in applications everywhere, with no luck. Maybe I'll do some volunteer work at the hospital. I kind of like it there."

"What kind of volunteer work?" Pam asked, suspiciously. "Following the interns around? Catering to their every little need?"

"Ha, ha," I said. "Actually, I'll be manning the magazine and book cart, as well as delivering flowers. Who knows? It might even turn into a real job if anything opens up in the gift shop. And," I said, snuggling up to Drew, "I'll be entertaining Drew with my outstanding charm and wit, every chance I get."

"Poor Drew," Don said, laughing. I threw a pillow from the lawn chair at him. It missed. "You might take up baseball practice too," he teased.

"I saw you talking to Susie's parents for quite a while, Jordan," Carrie said, changing the subject. "How is she?"

"They said she seems to be getting better," I told them all. "She's really a sweet girl. Drew and I plan on spending some of our summer getting to know her a little better, maybe taking her around to some parties and introducing her to more of the kids at school. She hasn't had much time for that in the past."

"Maybe we could plan another party just for her," Pam suggested cheerfully. "Sort of a getting-to-know-you party."

"Sounds good to me," I said. "But one party at a time." I looked at my watch. "And Mom and Dad will never let me have another one if I don't finish cleaning up this mess."

"Gee, I think that's our cue to be going now," Don teased.

"No you don't," Pam said, grabbing his arm.

"Coward," I said.

Pam held on tightly. "He's not going anywhere. We're

all in this together. Right gang?''

"Right," Don and Willy said halfheartedly. They looked so downcast at the thought of the chores ahead of them, I couldn't help laughing out loud.

Chapter Twenty-one

Drew stayed to help me with the last of the cleanup after everyone else had left. We folded the card table and stored it in the garage. We hosed off the patio. We washed and dried all the silverware and put it away. When we were done, we went back outside to enjoy the evening.

"Let's sit on the twins' swing set," I suggested. It was old and rusted, but the swings still worked.

"Mine creaks," Drew complained.

"Picky, picky."

He swung slowly. "Summer's in the air," he said.

"I know. I can smell it." I took a deep breath. "Three whole months with no school. What heaven."

"Look at the stars, Jordan."

I held onto the swing and threw my head back. The sky was black except for the millions of shimmering stars that glistened in the night. "Star light, star bright, first star I see tonight . . ." I let my voice trail off.

"Don't stop," said Drew.

"I wish I may, I wish I might, have this wish I wish tonight."

"Do you have a wish, Jordan?"

"Can't tell you," I teased. "If I tell you, it won't come true."

"If your wish is the same as mine, it can come true."

I wish for this night to never end. For more self-confidence. For a singing voice. For Susie to get better. For Carrie and Pam to always be my friends. For Chinese food twice a week for the rest of my life. And for Drew to—

"Jordan." Drew was talking to me, but his head was thrown back and he was staring at the stars. "Jordan," he said again. "In the fall I'll be starting college and I'm not sure what that will mean for us." He stood up and walked over to me. "But for now, for the summer, I was hoping that, well, that maybe you'd go steady with me."

(It's true. Wishing on a star does work. Thank you, star.)

I stood up. "Yes, I'd like that. I'd like that a lot."

He pulled me close to him and leaned down to kiss me. "I'll have to work this summer at the auto shop, but we'll still have the weekends and evenings to do things."

"We could go to the beach," I suggested.

"And maybe my folks would let you come camping with us," he said.

It sounded like fun, but I wasn't sure my parents would approve.

"Do you like to hike?" he asked.

"No."

"Oh."

"What else don't you like to do?"

He might as well know now. "Ski," I said. "I have a terrible sense of balance."

"Oh. I love to ski."

"I know," I said.

"Well, we won't have to worry about that till winter."

(Terrific. That gives me six months to become coordinated.)

"Drew? There's something else you should know. I didn't really want to be in ROP. It was sort of an accident. I don't like bed pans."

He laughed. "Jordan, no one *likes* bed pans."

"I know that, but to be truthful, I'm not sure I even like medicine. I like the idea of being a doctor, of being *someone*."

"Jordan," he said tenderly, "you *are* someone already. Someone very special."

"But the problem is, hardly anyone knows it and I want everyone to know it." There. It was out.

"It's only important that *you* know it," he said. He kissed the top of my nose.

"Drew," I said slowly, "do you think I'd be any good at electronics?"

His laugh echoed in the night air. It was a good laugh. A warm laugh. It hit the stars above and bounced back down again.

*   *   *

Long after he had gone, that laugh reverberated in my head. I looked out my bedroom window into the same sky that Drew and I had shared earlier. He was right. I could do or be anything.

I hugged Julius close. Maybe I'd be a veterinarian, saving wild elephants in darkest Africa.

Julius's worn shaggy coat felt familiar in the dark. Or a toymaker. I could make a million Juliuses for a million kids just like me.

"Good idea, Julius?" I asked him softly.

But wise old Julius didn't answer. He remained silent and approving. As always.